wonderstorm

© 2020 Wonderstorm, Inc. The Dragon Prince™,
Wonderstorm™ and all related character names are trademarks
of Wonderstorm, Inc. Used under license.
All rights reserved.

All rights reserved. Published by Scholastic Inc.,
Publishers since 1920. SCHOLASTIC and associated logos are
trademarks and/or registered trademarks of Scholastic Inc.

Library of Congress Cataloging-in-Publication Data available

ISBN 978-1-338-60356-9

10 9 8 7 6 5 4 3 2 1   20 21 22 23 24

Printed in the U.S.A.   23

First printing 2020

Book design by Betsy Peterschmidt

Cover and frontispiece artwork by Kelsey Eng

Map artwork by Francesca Baerald

THE
DRAGON
PRINCE

BOOK ONE: MOON

WRITTEN BY **AARON EHASZ &**
MELANIE McGANNEY EHASZ

CREATED BY **AARON EHASZ &**
JUSTIN RICHMOND

SCHOLASTIC INC.

PROLOGUE

L ong ago, Xadia was one land, rich in magic and wonder. In the old days, there was only the deep magic, which came from the six primal sources:

The Sun.

The Moon.

The Stars.

The Earth.

The Sky.

The Ocean.

Every living creature in Xadia was born with the gift of magic, a spark inside connected to one of the six primal sources. From the greatest dragon to the smallest insect, magic flowed in their veins.

But humans were different. Humans were flawed. They were born without this gift. Back in ancient times, the humans struggled to survive in the world, while the Xadian creatures thrived. Many humans perished from starvation; others died fighting one another over the scarce resources.

Unicorns were always the most selfless of the Xadian beings. There came a time when, filled with pity, they desperately wanted to help the struggling humans. After all, it was not the humans' choice to have been born without magic.

But the First Elves were wary. They warned the unicorns that kindness was not always returned with kindness; it would be a mistake to trust the species. After all, if humans were supposed to use magic, they would have been born with it.

However, the unicorns' compassion ran deep, and they could not be convinced. So, despite the elves' warning, the unicorns bestowed the ways of magic onto the humans. They gifted a few wise humans with powerful orbs called primal stones, which contained vast magical energy. Then they taught them to draw runes to attract and focus the stones' power, and to speak the ancient words used by dragons to release that energy as magical spells.

Finally, humans had the ability to take care of themselves and end their own suffering. They fed their hungry, cared for their poor, and healed their sick. As they thrived, they elevated humankind in other ways, learning about the world and the stars and the arts. They created songs and poetry and other beautiful things.

But the elves were right about one thing: Humans were unpredictable. While most were good, some were not. One human mage discovered a new way to use magic that was swift and facile but also dangerous and intense. This method used the essence within magical creatures themselves to unleash incredible power. Some called it new magic or the seventh source—but it came to be known as dark magic.

Dark mages and their followers began to hunt and poach magical creatures throughout Xadia, for they needed fuel for their spells: a griffin's talon, a feather from a moon phoenix, any part of a creature where magic was concentrated. Perhaps the most valuable and sought-after prize of all was a unicorn's horn. Eventually, the humans hunted the unicorns until they disappeared completely from Xadia.

The elves and the dragons were disgusted and outraged by what they saw. They were convinced the annihilation of humans was necessary and inevitable.

But at the last moment, a daughter of the elven leader proposed the Merciful Compromise. She asked that humans be allowed to move and settle the lands to the west. Beneath a half moon, the Dragon Queen, who was called Luna Tenebris, rendered judgment that was both cruel and kind. Humans were cast out, but they were spared.

And so, the continent was divided in two.

—*Aaravos of the First Elves*

MOON

Once there was a tribe who worshipped the Great Moon, a beautiful silver disc in the sky.

But one day, the righteous leader looked up and saw that half the moon was gone. "It's been stolen!" he cried.

The people were enraged. A war party traveled to the village of the neighboring tribe, whom they did not trust.

But the other leader saw things differently. "We stole nothing. The moon is not a silver disc, it is a silver leaf." She pointed to the sky, as proof. "This is the moon, and it is our moon."

The leaders each accused the other of lying, and soon the two tribes were at war. Many people died.

One night, both tribes found themselves lost in darkness. The moon had completely vanished. All the people were frightened, until a child spoke up.

"Don't you see?" the child asked. But the adults could see only darkness. Children do not see with just their eyes; they see with their hearts. "We all live under the same moon."

Finally understanding, the people stopped fighting.

And the moon smiled.

CHAPTER 1
ECHOES OF THUNDER

Torrents of rain poured down the high castle walls in the kingdom of Katolis. The raindrops sounded like pebbles beating against the pane-glass windows. Black storm clouds swirled in the sky, flickering with silent lightning.

Wrapped in a soft blanket, Ezran settled into his four-post bed, his unruly brown hair splayed over his pillow. Ezran's room was as messy as any eight-year-old's, but the room itself was grand and royal. The walls and floor were made of finely wrought stone, and the antique wooden furniture boasted delicate carvings of animals and forest scenery. Candles flickered, casting peaceful shadows across the walls.

The brightest light in the room emanated from Bait, Ezran's pet glow toad. This furless creature slept curled in the nook of

Ezran's elbow; he was the size of a cat but not nearly so cuddly. He kept his slick yellow-and-blue lizard skin close to his master's side, breathing in sync with the boy.

"Knock, knock! May I come in?" A voice rang from just outside Ezran's door.

"You're the king! I don't think you have to ask," Ezran called back.

King Harrow stepped into the room.

"Kings don't have to ask, but dads do," he said, winking at Ezran. He gave Bait a light pat as he sat on the edge of the bed.

The tiny monster grumbled a complaint, but secretly appreciated the affection. Bait was a loyal pet, but like most of his species, he was perpetually grumpy, a consequence of the fact that just about every wild animal larger than a glow toad considered glow toads delicious.

The king reached up and adjusted Ezran's covers. "Are you comfy cozy?"

"Comfy cozy," Ezran said. "You can sing now."

In a soft voice, the king sang the same lullaby he had repeated nearly every night since Ezran's mother died when he was an infant.

"The Sun is down, and the Moon is high.
Baby yawns wide with a sleepy sigh.
The Sky fills up with Stars that blink.
Baby's eyelids start to sink.
The Ocean kisses the Earth good night.
The waves say hushhh . . . little babe, sleep tight."

Ezran smiled. "I love that you still sing that to me. Even though it's for little kids, it makes me happy."

"Good," the king answered.

"Will you still sing it to me when I'm grown-up? I want you to."

"If you still want me to, then yes."

"Even when I'm king? You have to promise me that you'll still sing to me."

Harrow hesitated but then answered, "I will always watch over you, even when you are king."

He leaned over and pressed a warm kiss into Ezran's forehead. This was always the moment Ezran yawned, feeling so sleepy, so suddenly.

"Good night, sweet prince," Harrow said on his way to the door. He paused at the adjoining room. "And good night, Callum."

Ezran's older half brother, Callum, sat by an easel in the connecting room. He had a blanket draped around his shoulders and a gloved hand wrapped around a mug of tea. He sketched rapidly by the candlelight.

"'Night!" Callum answered without looking up from his drawing. He liked King Harrow, and he appreciated everything the king had done for him since his mother died, but the king wasn't Callum's dad. Sometimes the good-nights felt awkward.

Harrow slipped out, closing the door behind him.

Callum continued sketching. The fourteen-year-old could draw anything he had seen in perfect detail, even if he'd only seen it for an instant. But this sketch was from his imagination—a fantastical creature that was part giraffe, part alligator. Callum thought to himself that the "girrafigator" might look awkward, but it literally had a thick skin if anyone tried to tease it. And besides, if it needed to teach one of its tormentors a lesson, having a long neck that culminated in sharp teeth and powerful jaws might come in handy.

CRASH!

A sudden clap of thunder startled Callum from his thoughts.

"Callum!"

"It's okay, Ez," Callum called. He put down his pencil and went over to his kid-brother's bed. "It's just a thunderstorm. Nothing to be afraid of. Go back to sleep."

"I wasn't scared," Ezran said. "Bait was scared."

At the sound of his own name, Bait looked up with a frown and turned a deep shade of red. He did not appreciate any suggestion of cowardice on his part. He'd met many a glow toad in his day and knew that he was in the bravest five percent. Or at least the bravest ten percent.

But Bait could never stay angry at Ezran for long. His color faded as he fell back to sleep.

Lightning flashed, and the elves saw the human soldier patrolling the royal forest. The young man was on high alert, his eyes darting left and right as he scanned the thicket.

Rayla, the youngest of the team of elves, rubbed the handles of her blades with her long elven fingers. Did the soldier realize they were watching from the brush? Could he know that his very existence hung in the balance?

If the elves' leader, Runaan, gave her the signal, Rayla would take the soldier's life. She'd have no choice. She was an assassin, after all, and a fine one at that. She was swift with her blades and nimble on her feet. She could run and jump through the tall trees as well as any of her elders. Rayla would do anything Runaan asked of her.

Walk away, Rayla chanted in her mind, as if she could will the young soldier to leave his post. *Don't see us. Go home.*

The elves' mission had little to do with this particular human. He was just an annoyance on the journey to their true targets. They'd leave him alone if they could. But if the soldier spotted them . . . Rayla tried to stop thinking about it.

"Is anyone there?" the soldier called out into the darkness. He sounded confident, maybe even brave, and Rayla knew this did not bode well for him.

The elves stayed still. Rayla held her breath. One second passed. Then another.

"Declare yourself, in the name of King Harrow!" the human shouted.

Just a few more seconds of silence, Rayla thought to herself. *A few more seconds, and he'll realize it was nothing and keep moving.* Could the soldier hear her pounding heart?

Another flash of lightning brightened the sky, and the human's eyes grew wide. There was no question about it now. He had seen them.

He fired an arrow from his crossbow in their general direction, then turned on his heel and raced away.

In the blink of an eye, Runaan signaled with an almost imperceptible nod of his head.

Did he nod at me? Rayla wondered. No one else flinched. *Yes, he must have chosen me. Now I am death for this soldier.*

Her training kicked in, all the actions and reactions she had practiced endlessly became instinct in this moment, and she sprinted after her prey. Killing this human was her duty now, nothing more.

The soldier ran down the path as fast as a human could, his bulky cloak flapping in the wind, his clunky weapons slowing him down.

But Rayla was a creature of the woods. She leaped from tree branch to tree branch, her feet barely grazing the bark before she sprang to her next perch. She soared over the forest, always anticipating the target's next move. Faster and faster Rayla pursued, closing in on the soldier with each leap. The rain stung her cheeks. The putrid smell of the storm overwhelmed her senses. She'd never felt more alive.

The target was just out of reach now.

Rayla paused on a branch, her violet eyes narrow and sparkling in the dark woods. Then she leaped to the ground behind the soldier.

The soldier whipped around, but Rayla was already back in the darkness. She watched as he swung his crossbow wildly.

Get out there! Rayla told herself.

Before she could rethink it, she burst from the shadows and delivered a swift kick to the human's chest. He tumbled down a ravine into a river of mud. Rayla followed.

At the bottom, the soldier tried to fight, but it was pointless; Rayla had her blades at his neck in an instant.

"Please!" he begged. His panicked eyes took in her intricate weapons.

Do it now! Rayla thought. *Hesitation is torture, not mercy…* A swift execution was the only kindness she could offer.

The soldier was peering up at her now, searching for her face beneath the hood of her cloak.

"Who are you?" he asked softly.

Another flash of lightning. The target's face was illuminated for a moment, but a moment was all it took. Rayla saw the soldier's fear. She saw his sadness. She could almost hear his thoughts: *I'm going to die. I'm going to die.*

But she also saw his love for life and the promises it held for him—promises she would sever with her blades. She let her grip on her weapons loosen ever so slightly.

The soldier took his chance and crawled backward in the mud. Then he ran.

Rayla dropped her arms to her sides and hung her head, her will melted in the storm. Why was she so weak?

She stood still as a statue while the target made his escape.

CHAPTER 2
OLD SECRETS AND NEW SECRETS

Dawn shimmered over the damp forest. Birds chirped in the pink early-morning light. But inside the castle walls, the mood was still stormy.

Viren, the high mage, stood in front of an ornate mirror and grimaced in frustration. He traced one of the golden runes around its edges with a single, deliberate finger. If only he could unlock the secrets of this magical glass!

But the only revelation was his reflection—stern, tall, and finely dressed. His perfectly polished hair and clenched jaw made a silent mockery of his desire to know the mirror's secrets. His intuition told him the mirror would offer power—power to protect himself, his family, and the kingdom. But though he'd possessed the mirror for months, he'd yet to uncover any of its mysteries.

Viren glanced at the stack of leather-bound tomes on his desk. None of his spells or potions had divulged the mirror's secrets. Was it possible this was nothing but a mirror?

No, he scolded himself. If the Dragon King and Queen kept the mirror in their lair, next to where they slept, it could not be ordinary. It simply could not be! And if it was an ordinary mirror, it would not have called to him so strongly that day—called to him on a level so deep, he had seized the mirror from the great heights of the Storm Spire and carried it all the way back to the castle from Xadia.

He wasn't defeated yet; he was just missing something, some crucial clue.

Viren took a deep breath and pushed his exasperation deep within himself, into the ever-growing tomb of regrets, grudges, and vendettas buried inside him. He had risen to challenges before; he would rise to this one too. Most of the mysteries of Xadia had already fallen away before his formidable magic abilities, after all. His forays into the treacherous world of dark magic had been costly, of course. He'd lost loved ones and money, even sacrificed some principles, but perhaps all this effort was finally starting to pay off.

BANG! BANG!

Urgent pounding on the study doors startled Viren out of his reverie. Who would dare disturb him at this early hour? He would quickly put an end to this impudence.

"And how can I help you?" Viren said as he swung open the door. His voice was soft and cold and dangerous.

The young soldier standing in the doorway trembled. He was wet and covered head to toe in mud. A stream of blood trickled down his cheek.

"You've interrupted me!" Viren said. "What is it? Speak up, would you?"

The soldier choked back a sob.

"Oh, for goodness' sake, get a hold of yourself, young man."

The soldier spit his words out before he could lose his courage.

"Lord Viren, I've seen something. Something terrible in the royal forest."

Viren took a long, hard look at the soldier. Although he wanted to dismiss the sniveling brat, there was something in his face that made Viren pause. This soldier had been shaken to his core.

"I was out on my patrol, you see, and then there was lightning, and I saw a group . . . a group of assassins. One of them chased me. She had blades twice the size of her arms. I thought for sure I was a goner. But somehow, I got away. The assassin—well, I think she may have decided to spare me. I ran straight to you."

The soldier paused, but Viren remained silent, scrutinizing him. The sheer terror in this young man's eyes presented a sort of puzzle, but his story was still missing a piece.

"They were Moonshadow elves," the soldier whispered.

"Moonshadow elves?" Viren asked. He gave the soldier a withering glance. "You think you escaped from Moonshadow elves? You know what's less likely than you eluding a

Moonshadow elf? The idea that one of those bloodthirsty creatures found it in her heart to 'spare' you. Of all the nonsense I've ever heard . . ."

"I—I know the story must sound far-fetched, sir," the soldier stammered. "But in that moment there was some strange connection between me and the elf. She had me cornered, and then . . . it was as if she felt bad for me. She stopped chasing, and I had the chance to run."

"All right, all right. I don't need to hear about some touchy-feely moment you had in the forest," Viren said. "Why don't you report back to your supervisor. It's clear you've had a good scare, but trust me, it couldn't have been Moonshadow elves."

With that, Viren slammed the door in the soldier's face. Moonshadow elves sparing the life of a human! He shook his head in disbelief.

And yet, the elves were an ever-present threat. They couldn't stand humans, especially not the ones who used dark magic. And they would never get over the death of the king of the dragons, that much Viren knew. For a moment, he wondered if killing the Dragon King had been wise after all. But then again . . .

"I had no choice about it!" he shouted to the walls.

What if this soldier was right and elven assassins were nearby? It would make a certain amount of sense. If the queen of the dragons planned to avenge her husband by killing King Harrow, she wouldn't send a huge army, would she? She would send a band of the deadliest assassins in Xadia.

Viren walked over to his desk and flipped open a book of ancient charts and maps. He thumbed through the chapters until he reached the stages of the moon. What he saw was disconcerting. Perhaps it was a coincidence?

But the sinking feeling in his stomach told him it was not—if Moonshadow assassins were going to attack, they would do so on the night of a full moon. In just a few hours, they would be at the height of their powers.

Dread crept through Viren's limbs. Everyone knew the legends. Under a full moon, Moonshadow elves would be virtually unstoppable.

He grabbed a velvet cloth and flung it over the magic mirror— its secrets would have to wait for another day.

Moments later, he was striding through the dimly lit halls of the castle. As high mage, it was his job to conjure up creative solutions. There must be a way for him to stop these assassins . . . or at least a trick to send them off course. He considered possible strategies as he climbed the spiral staircase to King Harrow's tower. Near the top though, he braced himself for his immediate obligation: telling his closest friend that his life was in danger.

A guard outside the king's chamber informed Viren that the king was still sleeping, but Viren brushed past. He yanked Harrow's curtains open, then stood over his bed.

"And a good morning to you, Viren," Harrow said, rubbing the sleep from his eyes. "Didn't I tell you that if you ever woke me this early again, I'd have you executed?"

The king arched an eyebrow in the direction of the high mage, but the look on Viren's face put an end to all joking.

Rayla trudged toward camp, dragging her feet slower than she thought possible. Runaan would have expected her back by now. How would she tell him she wasn't only late, she'd also failed at her task?

Runaan had mentored her since she was just a wee elf. He'd trained her, drilled her, and encouraged her as she developed into a young assassin. He'd told her a thousand times that she was special—that he'd never put so much energy into someone who didn't have the spark she did. Now she would have to tell him he'd been wrong. He had wasted years grooming a protégé who empathized with the humans.

Rayla choked back sobs as she pictured the scene. Runaan's large, sincere eyes would fill with disappointment. He didn't deserve this, to be dishonored this way.

And the others—they would laugh at Runaan for having had faith in her. They'd told him she was too young for this assignment.

Rayla took a deep breath. Maybe her failure wouldn't matter once they'd finished the mission. After all, they hadn't come for that young soldier. As long as they assassinated the king and the prince, no one would care that one silly human didn't die.

And maybe Runaan wouldn't even ask if she had completed the kill—it would be assumed. But would her eyes give away her cowardice? She would have to keep her head down.

Rayla came to a stop just outside camp. The other assassins were quietly pitching tents and readying their weapons. Runaan sat cross-legged on a rock, meditating.

Get it over with, Rayla told herself, but her feet seemed stuck. She ran her fingers over a nearby bush, letting the leaves calm her thoughts.

One leaf, two leaves, three leaves. Runaan had taught her that a good assassin uses all their senses, including their sense of touch. *One berry. Another berry.*

Rayla gasped.

She knew she couldn't lie to Runaan. But it wouldn't really be lying if he came to his own conclusions, would it? If Runaan assumed she made the kill, she wouldn't have to dishonor him with a lie, right?

She plucked a single berry from the bush and squeezed it between her thumb and forefinger. Bloodred juice oozed out. Yes, this would work.

Rayla grabbed handfuls of berries and smashed them onto her blades. Scarlet liquid trickled off the weapons.

When both blades were dripping, she threw her shoulders back, looked straight ahead, and strode into camp.

Rayla didn't say a word as she passed Runaan; she didn't even make eye contact. But she tilted her blades in his direction. Her heart pounded in her chest.

"Well done, Rayla," Runaan said.

She glanced his way and gave a brief nod. It wasn't a lie; it was Runaan's mistake.

When the others noticed Rayla return, they nodded respectfully but stayed out of her way. They knew it was Rayla's first assassination, and they believed she'd succeeded. They also knew what it was to take a life. They knew it wasn't easy.

Rayla sat down and wiped her blades, the guilt of her deception heavy in her stomach.

CHAPTER 3
THE LAST NORMAL MORNING

*M*enacing, Callum thought. *The royal trees cast the most menacing shadows.* Callum loved drawing in the castle courtyard—the light was always perfect— but today, the shadows were catching his attention.

He pulled his sketchbook and pencil from his shoulder bag and started a quick sketch. He drew rapidly, glancing between the shadows and the page. The shadows of the branches on the courtyard stones seemed as stiff as skeletons. Where was the life?

He turned to a new page in his sketchbook, but a long shadow of a figure crept onto the paper, obscuring the leaves. Callum recognized the broad shoulders and thick neck, the full battle armor. The high mage's son, Soren, loomed over him.

"Hey, that's pretty good work, Step-Prince Callum," Soren

said. "But it's time to stop messing around. You have to work on your swordsmanship, and I have to teach you the skills." Soren clapped Callum on the back, sending his sketchbook and pencil flying. "Hopeless though that may be."

"Right. Of course, Soren," Callum said. He scrambled to pick up his belongings. His world had changed ever since his mother had married a king half a lifetime ago and turned him into a prince. No more mornings spent languishing in the sunshine, inventing characters and drawing out their details.

Now Callum had obligations. Responsibilities. Being a prince meant horseback riding, training with swords, strategic thinking, and learning the history of Katolis. Callum had struggled with all these subjects, but he kept trying because he loved his stepdad, King Harrow. He worked hard memorizing the names of old battles, long and odd names like the Battle at Berylgarten and Fortnight's Stand at Hinterpeak. Why couldn't battles have simpler names? If Callum ever got to name a battle, he would give it a simpler, more straightforward name—like Jenny. *Jenny would be a fine name for a battle.*

SNAP. SNAP. Soren snapped his fingers in front of Callum's eyes.

Right. Sword lessons. Callum turned to Soren, who launched into teacher mode.

"Today, we are going to focus on the art of—"

"Art!" Callum said. "Finally, something I'm good at."

"Right," Soren said. "If you had let me finish, you would know that we're going to focus on the art of defense."

"Well, if you want, you can draw your sword, and I can *draw* my sword." Callum held up his pencil when he said *draw* the second time and smiled at his own joke.

Soren blinked twice, and then continued without acknowledging Callum's joke. Callum was used to this.

"The art of defense is critical in sword fighting," Soren said. He leaned on the wooden training sword as he spoke, then hoisted it into the air.

"Parrying is about angle, motion, anticipation." He whipped the sword back and forth and punctuated each word with a stab at an invisible enemy.

"Misjudge your opponent, and it's over." Soren tapped Callum on the forehead with the dull side of the sword.

Callum sighed. Although Soren hadn't taken after the high mage in the ways of dark magic, Viren's only son was quite the physical specimen. He was tall, strong, and athletic, with golden-blond hair that always fell perfectly into place. He wore polished armor and carried a sword everywhere—a real sword, not the wooden kind that Callum had to practice with. At this moment, Soren had removed his real sword from its scabbard and was admiring the silver blade in the sun.

"It almost looks like it's glistening," Soren said. "Don't you think so, Step-Prince? Isn't this sword glistening?"

"Yes, very nice," Callum said. He put down his artist's bag. Soren was everything a prince was supposed to be. Pity his mind wasn't as sharp as his weapon.

"All right, let's get to it!" Soren tossed the practice sword to

Callum, who promptly dropped it. Soren rolled his eyes.

Callum retrieved the sword and lifted it in front of his face. Then he closed his eyes; it's not like he ever did any better with them open.

He swung the sword wildly, and it came into contact with Soren's. Still swinging, Callum backed up, but this time his weapon touched only air, and Soren's poked him in the chest.

"You're dead," Soren said calmly. Callum opened one eye.

"Yeah, but not if I was wearing armor, right?"

"Doesn't matter," Soren said. "Even if you were wearing the rarest, most elite armor forged by Sunfire elves, you'd be super dead."

"I'm awful at this." Callum rubbed the spot on his chest Soren had struck.

"Yup!" Soren said cheerfully. "But you have to practice anyway, because that's what's expected of a prince...I mean step-prince."

Callum stared at Soren but didn't say anything. The guy was always bringing up the fact that he wasn't King Harrow's "real" son. But the king was the only parent Callum had left; he could barely remember his biological father.

And his mother, Queen Sarai...Well, it was getting to be a long time since she had died.

Callum was about ready to give up sword practice when Claudia walked by, her head bent over a book.

Claudia was Soren's younger sister. Although she was less than a year older than Callum, he had always found her sophisticated, worldly, and enchanting. He figured the book she was reading had something to do with magic. She studied it with her father, and Callum knew she was very talented.

In fact, her love of magic was one of the things that made her weirdly fascinating to Callum, or rather, weird and fascinating. When he was with her, Callum always felt a light, persistent fluttering in his stomach, like a moon-crazed moth was trapped in his intestines.

Claudia had on her long black dress with the delicate golden edges sewn at the hem today. Her straight black hair hung far down her back, the dyed purple tips nearly touching her waist.

Weird. And fascinating.

"Tap, tap," Soren said, bonking Callum on the head with his sword handle. "Anybody in there?"

"Wha— Oh yeah," Callum said. "Hi, Soren. You know what, can we try again with the swords? I think I'm ready now." He tried to glance in Claudia's direction super casually, as if he didn't care at all that she was there now, but as soon as he saw her lovely face, he could feel his cheeks flush. Soren caught on.

"Ohhh. I see what's going on here."

For a second, Callum thought Soren was going to get angry, but instead he offered a conspiratorial smirk.

"Don't worry," he said. "I'll help. You come at me." He backed away and held up his sword.

Callum closed his eyes and bent down low. Then he ran at Soren, yelling like a maniac, and thrust his sword out. They clashed. Callum swung with all his might, and they clashed again. He swung once more, but this time hit air. When Callum opened his eyes, Soren was lying on the ground, clutching his side in mock agony.

"Oh, I've been stabbed!" Soren cried out.

Callum grinned. Sometimes Soren wasn't so bad.

"Stabbed so, so hard! By the stab-prince, Lord Stabbington."

Callum thought "stab-prince" had a nicer ring to it than "step-prince." And it was weirdly nice of Soren to help with Claudia like this, though he might have been laying it on a little thick.

"All right, Soren, you can get up now," Callum said.

"I cannot!" Soren yelled. "I'm only seventeen, but now I lay dying. Look! Spurt! Spurt!" Soren pointed at invisible blood exploding from his nonexistent wound. At the other end of the courtyard, Claudia laughed.

"Good job, Callum!" she said. "He deserves it."

While Soren continued to roll around on the ground, Callum went over to Claudia, who was still chuckling. He sat down next to her on a stone bench.

"What are you reading?"

"Oh, this?" Claudia rolled her eyes at the leather-bound book that must have been a thousand pages long. "It's just a bunch of boring magic stuff that I have to study. So boring!" She let out an exaggerated yawn.

"Boring? Are you kidding?" Callum said. "I'd love to learn magic. Magic is amazing!"

"I know, right?!" Claudia said. "I just didn't want to make you feel bad. Do you want to see something incredible?" Claudia looked both ways. "It's super rare, and my dad got it by . . . Well, it's a long story how he got it, but let me just show it to you."

Claudia slowly removed a spherical object from a covert pocket in her cloak. It was a clear glass ball filled with swirling dark blue air, miniature clouds, and tiny flickers of lightning. Callum had never seen anything like it.

"What is it?" he asked.

"It's called a primal stone," Claudia said. "It uses magical energy from one of the six primal sources." She handed it to Callum.

"Wow. What's inside?"

"It's a storm. A real storm. Captured from the top of Mount Kalik. I can channel its power to do spells with runes. Watch this." Claudia nudged Callum to look at Soren, who was primping in the reflection of his shield. She held up the primal stone and traced a rune shape in the air. As her fingertips moved, arcs of light formed, creating the glowing curves of the ancient, powerful symbol. Inside the glass orb, the miniature storm seemed to churn and change, and it pulsed with stronger and brighter forks of lightning.

"Aspiro!" Claudia said.

All at once, the shiny rune disappeared, and Claudia blew a windy swirl from her mouth. She directed the air in Soren's direction; it tousled his perfectly coiffed hair. Soren turned to his tormenters.

"Were you just trying to mess up my hair?"

Claudia shrugged.

"Well, it didn't work," Soren continued. "You just gave it even more volume."

Callum laughed. "That was amazing. What else can you do?"

Claudia began drawing another rune, but Callum felt a tap on his shoulder. It was a serious-looking guard.

"Prince Callum," the guard said. "The king needs to speak with you urgently."

Meanwhile, in the depths of the castle, Ezran and Bait went about their morning routine.

"What do you think Barius is baking this morning?" Ezran asked Bait. They were sitting in one of the castle's many secret tunnels. Most people (and glow toads) didn't even know about the tunnels, but together, Ezran and Bait had developed a keen talent for locating and opening false walls. This morning's secret passage was near the kitchen; buttery aromas wafted above their heads.

Bait blinked his amphibian eyes and licked his lips. He was pretty sure he smelled their most favorite treat.

"Yeah, I think I smell jelly tarts too!" Ezran said.

He peered out of the metal grate at the end of the passage. Sure enough, Barius was placing a tray of fresh tarts on the table.

Not yet, not yet . . . Ezran thought. He knew from experience that he needed to time these things just right. Even though Barius baked hundreds of tarts a day—even though he could bake tarts in his sleep—he always made such a fuss when he caught Ezran swiping a tart. In fact, Ezran thought it was funny that Barius made the sweetest, sugariest treats in all the kingdom, because the baker himself was a royal sourpuss.

After an eternity, Barius finally waddled off to work on something else.

Ezran slowly slid the grate to the side. Then he scampered to the tray and snagged a piping-hot tart.

The very first bite scorched his mouth, but he continued to sink his teeth into the buttery crust. Some things were worth a sore tongue.

"Prince Ezran! I caught you!" Barius yelled from across the kitchen.

Ezran froze, but then took another enormous bite. "Ohhh. I'm sorry, Barius. I thought these were the throwaways."

"Throwaways? Did you see the perfect golden crust? The impeccable triangular shapes? Why are you still chewing? Put that down!"

"I mean, now this one is a mess-up," Ezran said. "I've already bitten into it; you might as well let me have it."

Barius raised his bushy gray eyebrows in disbelief at the young prince's cheekiness. People around here didn't appreciate him nearly enough. Running a castle kitchen was no small feat. The only reason it ran so smoothly was because of the military-like procedures he'd put in place for himself. He started up the oven at six o'clock sharp every morning. He baked tarts, cookies, and other treats in batches of exactly twelve. He distributed them in batches of twelve too. One could not request fifty tarts for a party. It could be only forty-eight or sixty.

(Someday, he wouldn't have to tell party organizers that rule over and over again.)

But he never compromised quality for quantity. He was exacting in all his measurements, precise with his whipping techniques. And for his jelly tarts, he used only the finest imported jams. He carefully whisked the batter for exactly eight minutes. He shaped each tart into a perfectly equilateral triangle.

And now the prince had gobbled up his precious creation. The entire batch would have to be thrown out. Eleven tarts simply would not do. He looked toward the ceiling and launched into a rant about this new generation of disrespectful children.

But Ezran was watching closely. Once he was certain the baker was completely immersed in his list of grievances, Ezran gave Bait the signal: He wiped jelly off his face with the back of his left hand.

Never one to take a chance when it came to sweets, Bait immediately flicked his enormous tongue out and lapped up three tarts from the tray. He stuffed them in his cheeks for safekeeping. Could he risk another swipe? He flicked his tongue again, but the tarts stuffed in his cheeks made it awkward. He was slow. Too slow.

Barius tore off his chef's hat and charged at Bait. The glow toad found his speed again. This wasn't the first time he'd been chased around the kitchen.

Ezran smiled. This morning was going quite well. He scooped the rest of the tarts into his shirt and escaped through the secret passage. He and Bait would meet later to divide their spoils.

Callum arrived at the throne room doors out of breath. He was surprised to find Ezran there, holding Bait and anxiously eating jelly tarts.

"So, he wants to see you too?" Callum asked. "I wonder what this is about."

Ezran shrugged. "Should we go in?"

The boys pushed open a heavy door and peeked inside. The throne room, with its soaring ceilings and stone columns, was one of the most intimidating places in the castle; the sheer size could make even a prince feel insignificant. A long crimson carpet ran from the entrance to the foot of the hand-carved throne that had occupied this room for centuries. Standing candelabras cast shadows over the marble floors.

In the middle of the great hall, the king, Lord Viren, and a number of attendants stood huddled around a long table. A three-dimensional map of the five human kingdoms and Xadia was laid out before them. It looked like a table game, with pieces representing the various armies and miniature terrain delineated by kingdoms.

But this was not a game; this was the place where the powerful discussed trade routes, treaties, and other things of international importance. In more troubled times, the table was used to devise battle strategies. King Harrow stood over the table, his brow furrowed. But as soon as he saw Callum and Ezran, his expression filled with joy and delight.

"Boys!" the king called out. He hurried toward the children, a glowing smile on his face. "I am so glad to see you." He gave each boy a huge bear hug.

"Hi, Dad!" Ezran said.

King Harrow put one hand on each of the boys' shoulders. "I've got a big surprise for you. You two are going on a trip!"

"We are? Where?" Callum asked.

"You're going to the Banther Lodge! And you're leaving today," the king said. He was all smiles, but Callum detected a worried look in his eyes.

"But, it's spring," Callum said. "That's the winter lodge."

"Yeah, and why are we leaving today?" Ezran wanted to know. "What will we do? Everything fun there has to do with snow or ice." His voice had gotten a little whiny.

"Well . . . Use your imagination," the king said. "Maybe you could invent new versions of your favorite winter games, but using dirt and rocks. I know! You could build a dirtman. You know, like a snowman, but made of . . . dirt!"

Ezran gave the king a suspicious look. "You're acting weird. Is something wrong?"

"Nothing's wrong," the king answered. "Oh, I've got it! What about mudsledding? That could be a thing. Nothing weird about that!"

Callum shook his head. "Now you're just digging the hole deeper."

"Hole-digging contests! Now you've got it, Callum."

Callum looked at Ezran and then down at the ground. He

could tell that despite the king's cheer, something wasn't right. *I don't want to be rude to the king*, Callum thought, *but...*

King Harrow bent down so he could look into the boys' eyes. His expression changed, and he lowered his voice.

"Look, all kidding aside, this is something I need you to do. You'll leave before sundown—"

"But, Dad," Ezran interrupted.

"I don't want to hear any protests, Ezran. Go get packed."

The boys left quietly; it was clear to both that something was up.

"Why is he sending us away?" Ezran wondered as they walked down the hall. "He's acting weird. I'm worried."

"Everything's going to be fine, Ez. Try not to worry." Callum put a reassuring hand on Ezran's shoulder. "Why don't you go play while I start packing? Bait looks like he needs a little cheering up."

The glow toad was frowning, despite having eaten his share of jelly tarts. Ezran laughed.

"Bait always looks like that!" But he scooped up the glow toad, and the two scampered out into the courtyard just the same.

Callum decided to follow; he could use some fresh air. He watched his little brother play. He was just as worried about being sent away as Ezran, but he couldn't let the younger boy see his fear. For the life of him, Callum couldn't imagine what might be going on. Was there some important meeting of the human rulers that they needed peace and quiet for?

A voice coming from above him in the courtyard interrupted his thoughts.

"They must be set up somewhere at the base of the cliffs."

Callum turned to see where the voice was coming from. It was Viren, standing in front of an open window in the nearby tower. From the looks of it, he was giving orders to Soren.

Callum tuned his ears to the conversation but kept his eyes on Ezran. He thought he heard Viren say something about a secret camp. He was sure he heard Soren complaining. But was it possible Soren had just said *assassins*? Viren murmured something back before Soren's voice came ringing out in a loud shout: "Moonshadow elves will kill the king?!"

Callum gasped. Moonshadow elves?! It couldn't be.

He looked up instinctively and caught Viren's eye, then looked away, trying to pretend he hadn't overheard. The high mage closed the double windows with a furious slam.

It all made sense now.

Callum's stepfather's life was in danger, and he knew it. He and Ezran were being exiled to the Banther Lodge for their own protection.

Callum turned back to Ezran and Bait playing in the courtyard. He couldn't tell Ezran about this. And yet, how could he leave the castle now, when he knew what was at stake?

CHAPTER 4
NO TURNING BACK

Rayla sat nervously at camp, wondering if Runaan could read her mind.

It doesn't matter, she decided, as the sun moved lower in the sky. Whether or not she had spoken false words, she had deceived Runaan intentionally; she had lied to him. She would give anything now to complete the mission and make sure there were no consequences to the lie. Maybe then, in time, her deception would shrink and fade from her mind.

Runaan suddenly stood and shook himself from his meditative trance. He pointed at the sun, low in the sky; it was time for the binding ceremony.

Without a word, Rayla and the other elves followed Runaan into a small clearing and formed a circle. This was Rayla's first binding ceremony, but she'd heard many stories about the infamous ritual.

She knew Runaan would secure ribbon bindings around each assassin's arm, bindings that would supposedly grow tighter and tighter, slowly squeezing the life out of the assassins until the mission was complete.

But Rayla wasn't sure if she believed the lore. Could a flimsy piece of ribbon—even an enchanted one—really kill an elf who hadn't succeeded? There was no way to know; in the past century, the only assassins who didn't complete their missions had died trying. Their bindings became irrelevant.

Rayla took a deep breath. She was ready to be bound to this mission. She needed to be bound to this mission. She would make up for her mistake with the soldier by channeling every ounce of energy into the task at hand.

But it wasn't just her own mistakes Rayla was desperate to make up for.

This was her chance to rectify her parents' mistakes, their acts of cowardice that had shamed the community and Rayla. She would redeem herself, her parents, and get justice for Xadia. And she would make it happen all within the next twenty-four hours. All she had to do was follow Runaan and act decisively. She snapped to attention when Runaan addressed the assassins.

"Four full moons past, on the eve of the winter's turn, the humans crossed into Xadia and murdered the king of the dragons. Then they destroyed his only egg, the Dragon Prince. Tonight, we bind our lives to justice."

"My breath for freedom," said the first elf.

"My eyes for truth," said the second.

"My strength for honor," said the third in the circle.

"My blood for justice," said the fourth.

"My heart for Xadia," Rayla added. As she spoke the words, she knew her promise was true and would always be so.

Runaan walked from elf to elf with the long white binding ribbon in his hands. He stopped at each assassin and looped the ribbon around their wrists. One binding to represent the king's life; the other, the life of the crown prince. Runaan looked into the eyes of each assassin as he secured their bindings.

"Life is precious," he said. "Life is valuable. We take it, but we do not take it lightly." Runaan paused to let the gravity of their duty sink in.

He came to Rayla last. Runaan wrapped the final bindings, looking Rayla squarely in the eye. This was her chance to show him she was the assassin he'd raised her to be: trustworthy, unwavering, and deadly. She took a deep breath and then spoke in the fiercest voice she could.

"Moon reflects sun as death reflects life!"

Runaan nodded. They were words he had taught her many years ago.

The elves stood with their arms toward one another, tied together in formation. Rayla's heart skipped a beat.

Runaan stepped back and withdrew his long blades. In a split second, he had severed the bindings and released the elves from the circle.

Rayla stared at the newly created bands on her wrists as they glowed a bright white, then faded to normal. She thought she felt a small tingle and maybe a slight tightening of the bands. Was it just her imagination or could the enchantment be real?

Runaan pulled an arrow from his quiver and held it up for the assassins to see. Its tip was shaped like a strange and beautiful bird with a jeweled eye.

Rayla stared in awe—she'd heard about these magical arrows but had never seen one. Supposedly, the arrows would fly to their intended recipients no matter how many miles they had to travel or turns they had to take to get there.

"When it is done," Runaan said, "I will send a shadowhawk arrow with a blood-ribbon message to the queen of the dragons." Then he put the arrow back in his quiver.

Rayla nodded. That arrow would signal more than a completed mission. It would mark the end of years of strife between humans and Xadia. It would signal justice and resolution.

"We strike when the moon is highest," Runaan declared, dismissing them.

The elves dispersed to resume their preparations.

Rayla found a spot and sat down to sharpen her blades. She knew Runaan and the others would go after the king first; she decided she would go after the crown prince. She visualized the young warrior, spoiled by his riches and all his servants, raised to hate and kill elves. She would slither silently into the castle and locate him within minutes. She would whip out her blades and end his life so quickly, he wouldn't have a chance to fight or even feel fear.

Yes, that was the noblest approach. He may be a human, but he didn't deserve to spend his last moments in terror.

Rayla was gazing toward the castle when something caught her eye. *Is that a hummingbird?* she thought. *Or maybe a— Wait.*

Rayla stood up and walked closer to the small creature.

It can't be.

But the rapid flutter and its luminous green wings were unmistakable. It was an archangel lunaris, a Xadian moon moth.

"Runaan, look!" she called. She pointed to the moth. "I thought we only had those in Xadia."

Runaan's eyes widened.

"Runaan, what's wr—"

"They've used the moth to track us—the humans know we're here!" Runaan shouted.

The other elves looked up, panicked. Rayla's senses went on high alert. Was that the sound of approaching horses in the distance?

But Runaan acted fast. He grabbed the pendant he wore around his neck and extracted the rare Moon opal from inside. It glittered with primal Moon energy. He crushed the opal in his fist, letting light and sparkling dust burst from between his fingers.

"Mystica arbora!" He practically hissed the ancient Draconic words.

Almost instantly, Rayla felt herself transform. She tried to move her arms, but they were frozen out in front of her—frozen into the limbs of a forest tree. Though she knew the spell was merely an illusion, the transformation felt completely real.

Somehow, she could still use her eyes. The other assassins had transformed into trees as well, locked in position when Runaan cast the spell.

Just a few moments later, a group of humans arrived on horseback and gathered near the moon moth, which was resting on one of Runaan's branches. Rayla could tell by their armor that this was the king's guard. She held her breath . . . even though she no longer had a mouth or nose.

A knight, the apparent leader of the group, leaped off his horse and strutted over to the moth. The magical creature was flapping its wings vigorously, flying back and forth between the knight and the Runaan tree. But the knight seemed too dense to pick up the hint.

"Well, surprise, surprise," he said. "A magical moon moth is just as useless as a regular moth."

"Are you sure, sir?" asked one of the soldiers. "It seems to be trying to tell us something."

Rayla gasped. The soldier who had spoken was the very same young man she had allowed to escape this morning!

"Of course I'm sure," the knight said. "We'll have to wait for the elves to come to us."

The blond-haired knight climbed back onto his horse and galloped off, the group trailing behind him. But the young soldier lagged behind, staring long and hard at Rayla's tree.

Was he sensing something? Would he see through the illusion? Finally, he gave up and went off to catch up to the others.

The moment the horses were out of hearing range, the elves changed back into their natural forms. They all looked shocked—except for Runaan. He whipped his head around and glared at Rayla.

"You lied to me." His voice was soft, but the rage was unmistakable. "You let him go."

"Runaan, I'm so sorry." Rayla started to apologize. In the moment, she somehow felt both relieved that Runaan knew the truth and terrified that he might hate her. "The human—he looked up at me and I could see the fear in his eyes. How could I kill him? He'd done nothing to me!"

"You let him live," Runaan whispered, "but you've killed us all."

The impact of his words sank in, and Rayla realized the gravity of her mistake. Moonshadow elves were unstoppable assassins—once a target was set, its demise was certain. The only uncertainty was whether the assassins themselves lived or died while completing the mission. Runaan clearly believed this mission would now end in sacrifice.

Rayla looked up at her mentor, but all she saw in his ice-blue eyes was disappointment and anger.

"Runaan, she's betrayed us," said one of the other elves. "She's faltered."

"Yes, Runaan," another said, "We're all at risk now. No elf has done anything like this in recent history. You know what tradition says you have to do."

Rayla couldn't believe they were turning on her over this one mistake, a mistake made from compassion. She looked pleadingly at Runaan.

"Please, Runaan. I'll never let you down again." She wasn't certain, but she thought she saw his eyes soften just a little bit.

"Runaan, you know that weakness is an infection," the third elf said so angrily he was spitting. "You must cut it out!"

"I'm the leader, and you all will follow my lead," Runaan said. But he knew that the fellow assassins were right. It was his responsibility to make this mission succeed, and he could not falter because he felt a twinge of pity for young Rayla. Still, he hesitated.

"It's your duty to kill her, Runaan," the last elf insisted.

And she was right. It was the custom. It was the law.

Rayla could not believe she found herself in this position, facing a deadly consequence she had brought on herself. She knew Runaan cared for her deeply, but she had left him no alternative but to follow through and execute the law.

Runaan looked at his angry assassins and then at Rayla. When he spoke, his voice dripped with disgust.

"I'm not going to kill this infant. It was my mistake to bring her here. She's just a child—she's no assassin."

Somehow this caught Rayla off guard. "But Runaan . . ." Rayla had trained all her life to be an assassin. How dare he write her off as a mere child!

The other elves protested too.

"You must kill her!" someone shouted, and the others joined in with certainty.

"Rayla," Runaan said, "your punishment will be a child's punishment. You're off the mission. Go home to Xadia and play with the other children."

"Runaan, she can't be trusted," an elf said. "It's not just a matter of punishment; it's a matter of precision. She's a danger to us all."

Rayla felt tears well in her eyes. She'd never meant to betray the others.

"She has to die!"

"Please, Runaan!" Rayla shouted. "My heart for Xadia!" A sob escaped her lips.

Runaan stared into Rayla's eyes, unblinking, as the other elves jeered and yelled, pushing him to take action. Finally, Runaan roared at Rayla with the ferocity of a lion. She had never seen him so fierce, so terrifying.

She turned and bolted into the woods.

○

Rayla came to a stop near a tall oak tree. She didn't know how long she'd been running, only that she had never run that far or fast before.

"I'm sorry, Runaan," Rayla said to the forest. "I am so, so sorry."

She sank down against the tree, closed her eyes, and let the tears flow like she'd let her feet run.

When she had no more tears, she pulled herself up and took in her surroundings. The sun would soon set; the assassins would approach the castle, to a certain ambush by the castle army. Because of her, the mission would cost them their lives.

Unless...

Rayla wiped her face with the back of her hand and scrambled on top of a craggy rock. She could just make out the castle in the distance.

Runaan himself had said she was the fastest of the assassins. No one could soar across the forest like she could.

"I can fix this," Rayla said.

She straightened her shoulders and bowed her head. Then she leaped off the rock and ran headlong toward the destiny she had chosen.

CHAPTER 5
THE LETTER AND
THE SERPENT

Callum still couldn't believe what he'd overheard Viren say. He'd packed his things quickly but was now frantically pacing the halls trying to calm himself down. Was it possible he had misunderstood?

But the assassination threat explained why King Harrow was sending the princes off to the Banther Lodge in the middle of spring. It must be true. There really were skilled assassins coming for the king. For Callum's stepdad.

Suddenly, Callum realized there was no way he could go to the lodge. So what if he was a skinny kid who could barely swing a sword? Every single body standing in front of the king would offer some protection. And he wasn't a baby anymore—he was nearly fifteen years old and that was old enough to fight.

Certainly, he was too old to run away with his little brother and cower in the lodge building "dirtmen."

"I have to be brave," Callum whispered to himself. "For the king, and for my brother."

But what about Ezran? Callum had a feeling he would refuse to go to the Banther Lodge without his big brother.

Of course. That must be why King Harrow was sending them both away. Even though Ezran would be surrounded by dozens of guards at the lodge, the king would want Callum along to make his little brother feel safe. There was no other reason for King Harrow to send Callum. Except . . . except that maybe the king was trying to protect Callum too.

Callum was starting to see the sense in the king's plan. The king would be better able to focus if he knew the boys were safe. And the crown guard was strong, certainly strong enough to have a fighting chance against a small group of elves.

At the end of the hallway Callum knocked on the door to Ezran's room.

"Come on, Ez! Let's get moving, no time to waste," he yelled out. "It's almost sundown."

There was no response.

Callum got down on his knees and tapped open Bait's miniature glow toad door. (King Harrow had insisted on building the tiny door himself, though the royal carpenter had secretly made a few subtle adjustments.) Callum peeked through the opening into Ezran's bedroom.

But Ezran's room was empty. His traveling bag was lying on the floor, not yet packed.

"NO!" Callum pounded his fist on the door in frustration. Of course Ezran wasn't taking the trip seriously. He was probably still chatting with birds in the palace gardens.

But then the hairs on the back of his neck pricked up; he felt the presence of someone behind him.

"I'm so glad you're back, Ez!" Callum said, standing up.

"Ahem. Prince Callum."

Callum found himself facing the shoulder plates of an enormous, serious-looking guard. "Um, yeah, that's me," Callum said. "What's going on?"

"King Harrow would like to see you again," the guard said.

"Again? What for?" Callum asked.

"I do not know, sir. I am just the messenger."

"Did he seem like maybe he was, I don't know, mad at me about something?"

"He did not."

Callum was relieved. "Okay, great."

"That said," the messenger continued, "he's usually very even-tempered with me, always very appropriate. So he certainly could be reserving his anger until he sees you in person."

Callum gulped. Could King Harrow have already figured out that Callum lost his little brother?

"You wanted to see me?" Callum asked. He poked his head tentatively into the throne room, then slid the rest of his body through the ten-inch space he'd made between the doors. The great doors slammed shut behind him.

King Harrow turned. Worry lines creased his face.

"Prince Callum," he said gravely.

Callum trudged the length of the red carpet toward his stepfather.

"My King," Callum said, and made a short, formal bow.

King Harrow seemed suddenly uncomfortable. He reached his hand out in a hesitant but reassuring manner.

"No . . . please relax, Callum. I didn't mean for this to be so formal," he said.

"Okay," Callum said. But he stood with his back as straight and stiff as ever.

The king looked up at the vaulted ceilings and paused. Then he looked into Callum's eyes and smiled.

"Callum, I know I'm not your birth father, but I've always wanted you to feel comfortable around me. We are family. I want you to know that . . ." The king took a deep breath, his brow furrowed. "Forgive me. This isn't easy to say. So, the most important things I've written down."

From deep within his royal robes the king withdrew a parchment scroll and handed it to Callum. Callum turned the scroll over carefully. It was stamped with the official red wax seal of the King of Katolis.

"A letter for me?" Callum asked.

"Yes, it's a letter for you—and for your eyes only. You'll understand in time. I want you to break the seal when . . . Well, you'll know when."

"When you're dead," Callum burst out. "You think I don't know what's going on?"

King Harrow took a step back, his jaw slack with surprise.

"I heard about the assassins," Callum said.

The king bent down to look Callum in the eyes and put his hands on his stepson's shoulders. "War is full of uncertainty, Callum," he said softly. "I hope you won't have to open this letter, but we must be prepared."

"Why can't you just do something to stop the elves?" Callum asked, close to tears. "Can't you just make peace with them? You're the king."

"It's not that simple," King Harrow said.

"It seems pretty simple to me," Callum said, his frustration building. "The elves want to live. We want to live. Everyone agrees on at least *one* important point."

The king smiled. After all, his stepson was correct. "There are centuries of history, generations of wrongs and crimes on both sides. I know you don't want to believe it, Callum, but I'm responsible for some of those wrongs. And they cannot just be forgotten."

Callum stepped back. It was hard to imagine his warm, doting stepfather committing unforgivable acts, but here he was admitting to the unthinkable. What, exactly, had he done?

Callum desperately wanted to reassure the king, whose

shoulders bore the burden of whatever past choices he had made. But how could he tell this man, a king, that it was time to move on?

"I've done terrible things," King Harrow said. "I thought they were necessary at the time. But now I have many regrets."

"There has to be a way to make it right," Callum said. "Maybe you shouldn't focus so much on the past. Maybe the humans and the elves can find a way to move forward together."

"I admire your youthful optimism," King Harrow said. "But it's too late. What is done cannot be undone."

"You're the king!" Callum pleaded. "You can do or undo anything!"

Harrow chuckled bitterly. "The great illusion of childhood is that adults have all the power and freedom. But the truth is the opposite. A child is freer than a king."

Callum gave his stepfather a skeptical stare, but he knew King Harrow was the most stubborn king in the history of Katolis. If he believed he deserved some terrible fate, there was no changing his mind. Callum looked down at the scroll.

"I'm going to give this back to you this weekend, okay?" he said. "I'm not going to have to open this." He searched his stepfather's face for a sign that maybe, just maybe, there was a chance he would live through this night and everything would go back to normal.

But King Harrow shook his head stoically. "Take care of your brother, Callum," he said and turned away.

Callum knew this was his cue to leave. He trudged toward the doors wondering if this was the last time he'd see the only parent he had left.

From the moment King Harrow had married Callum's mom, he had raised Callum as his own son. And yet . . . Callum had never told him he loved him. He'd never called him "Dad" or even "Stepdad." The closer he got to the door, the more Callum's insides crumbled.

Don't cry, don't cry, he told himself. He couldn't cry here in the throne room; he had to show the king he was brave and strong. He paused before the door to collect himself. *Don't look back, don't cry.*

Suddenly, Callum felt the king's strong arms wrap around him. He shut his eyes and let his whole body relax into the embrace. A sob escaped his mouth. Warm tears were sliding down the king's face too.

Callum wrapped his own arms around King Harrow and squeezed tightly. He had to make this count.

When he looked up, he caught Viren standing awkwardly in the corner of the room. Harrow noticed him too.

"Uh, can I help you? That's a little creepy, Viren," King Harrow said. He let go of Callum.

Viren was clutching an intricately woven basket, a bunch of soldiers behind him.

"Sorry, I didn't want to interrupt your, uh, familial clasp," Viren said.

"It's called a hug, Viren," King Harrow said. Viren could be awkward sometimes.

"Yes, of course. My children and I do those as well. When the occasion calls for it," Viren said.

"Right. Well, I see you've brought me something," Harrow said, pointing at the basket. "Not a great day for a picnic, Viren."

"On that we agree," replied the high mage, raising his black, slanted eyebrows.

"Don't worry, I was just leaving," Callum said. He glanced back at King Harrow and caught one last, loving look before he slipped out through the door.

Viren waited pointedly for Callum to exit before he began to speak. "Soren and the others have returned to bolster your defenses," Viren told the king. "But the elves have eluded us. We will not find them by sundown."

"I'm afraid our forces won't be enough," King Harrow said, staring out the window. "I've accepted that tonight I may pay the price for our mistakes. The elves are flawless assassins. Once the moon is up, nothing will stop them."

"It's true, My King, Moonshadow elves are dangerous, elite fighters. Under a full moon, they'll become nearly invisible and able to penetrate any defense," Viren said. He placed his hand on the king's shoulder. "But don't give up just yet." He patted the wicker basket. Inside, something hissed and wriggled. "Claudia and I have come up with a, uh, creative solution."

King Harrow's eyes narrowed; he seemed unwilling to look in Viren's direction. "Call it what it is, Viren," he said. "Dark magic."

Viren stepped back, surprised at the venom in King Harrow's voice. "Yes."

"I've spent years going along with these 'creative solutions' of yours. And where has it gotten me?"

"I don't understand your hesitance," Viren said.

"I know you don't," the king said.

Viren thought fast. "Of course there have been tragedies and sacrifices over the years, but we never did anything that wasn't necessary. We secured the kingdom. And we saved many lives. On that note, there may be a way out of this situation we find ourselves facing tonight. Would you just hear me out?"

King Harrow remained silent.

"You are right about one thing. Moonshadow elves will find you, and they will kill you. But it doesn't have to be YOU." Viren paused for dramatic effect.

"Get on with it," King Harrow said. "I haven't got time for suspense."

Viren bristled, but continued. "In the black sands of the Midnight Desert there dwells a mysterious snake called the soulfang serpent." He drummed his long fingers on the wriggling basket. "The soulfang has an unusual diet. Its bite consumes the spirit of its prey. On our last journey into Xadia, I acquired a rather unique specimen of this snake."

Viren placed the basket on the floor and with a flick of his staff, removed the top with delicate precision. The body of a snake, long, black, and leathery, wrapped around Viren's staff. Viren held the staff at arm's length, filled with cautious respect for the frightening creature. There were glimpses of a flicking red tongue and gnashing white fangs.

Then, as it twisted about, the serpent revealed that it had not one but two heads growing out of a single body. The two-headed monster stared at King Harrow and rattled its tail. King Harrow took a step back.

"Two heads, two bites, two souls held at once!" Viren said. "And, through magic, I can switch your spirit with another. The Moonshadow elves will find the king's body, but your spirit will survive." Viren smiled. Surely, King Harrow would see the wisdom in this maneuver, this clever trick.

"No!" Harrow yelled. "I won't hide in the body of another while someone else dies paying the price for my decisions!"

Viren shook his head. The king could be so bullheaded. "That makes no sense, Harrow," Viren said. "Hundreds of men and women are ready to fall protecting you tonight, but you won't let one soldier sacrifice their life for you right now?"

"It's not the same," King Harrow said. "I would rather die a king than live as a coward."

"So, this is just about your pride," Viren said.

"No, I already told you the problem, Viren." King Harrow's voice rose in anger. "It's dark magic."

"Ohhhh. Yes, who wouldn't have a problem with dark magic?" Viren sneered. "It's clever, it's brilliant, it's practical. You are too stubborn to make use of the tools that are available to you. It will save your life, just as it has saved the lives of countless others."

"It's a shortcut," King Harrow snapped back. "We may not pay now, but we will pay the blood price eventually."

"Now you're starting to sound like *her*," Viren said with a smirk.

King Harrow stiffened at the mention of Queen Sarai. Before her death, the queen had harbored abundant misgivings about dark magic.

"Maybe I do sound like her," he said. "But, so what? Dark magic is dangerous. What do you think got us into this position?"

"You're not only bullheaded," Viren continued, his voice rising, "you're ungrateful."

"Should I be grateful that you destroyed that dragon's egg?" King Harrow asked, his voice heavy with sarcasm. He clasped his hands together in a mock prayer. "Thank you, Viren, for starting this unwinnable war. Thank you for angering the dragons and the elves so much that tonight they are here for my life!"

But Viren just shook his head. The ends would justify the means. Why couldn't the king understand that? "Destroying that egg saved our kingdom and maybe all of humanity," he said.

"It was just an egg!" King Harrow shouted.

"And it would have become the most powerful creature in the world!" Viren barked, finally losing his cool.

King Harrow seemed to realize he was getting nowhere. He sat down on a bench and dropped his head in his hands.

"What is done cannot be undone," Viren said. He lowered his tone in reconciliation. "I am offering you a path forward. Can't you see that? I understand your discomfort. You don't feel right trading your life for another's. But know this, every one of these men and women would gladly trade their life to save yours."

Viren indicated to the group of soldiers standing a few feet away. The soldiers shifted uncomfortably, though there was truth in what Viren said.

King Harrow picked his head up and scrutinized the high mage's expression. "Would you gladly trade your life, Viren?"

The question caught Viren off guard, and for once he was speechless. After a few long seconds of silence, he began to stutter an answer.

"My K-King . . . I . . ."

But it was too late.

"Get out," King Harrow said.

This time, Viren knew the discussion was over. He stuffed the serpent back into the basket, bowed, and exited the room in silence.

CHAPTER 6
THE ASSASSIN'S EDGE

Callum left the throne room resolved to do King Harrow's bidding. He would find Ezran and coax him to go to the Banther Lodge where they would both be safe. It wouldn't be easy, but Ezran trusted him.

The bigger challenge would be locating his little brother in the vast castle. His brother had an uncanny ability to mysteriously disappear at point A, only to reappear later at point B without anyone knowing how he got there. Callum traipsed down the corridors with his ears attuned to any scratches or scrapes inside the walls that might lead to a small boy and his pet glow toad.

And then, a sudden tingle jolted Callum's senses. Was that the shuffle of a foot on the castle rugs? A faint whiff of damp trees passed under his nostrils, and a shadow glinted in the corner of his eye. This wasn't Ezran playing a trick on him, he was fairly sure of that. It couldn't be a castle guard either—they weren't so slippery.

Callum did an about-face and called out. Maybe it was Ezran, after all?

"Ez? Is that you?"

But there was no response. He tried again.

"Hello?"

Something wasn't right. Callum flattened his back against a nearby wall and edged toward the corner where he'd seen the shadow. He couldn't decide if he was following some mysterious presence or if it was following him. He faked a turn around the corner, quickly rotating back the way he came.

"AHH!" Callum nearly dropped his backpack—he was face-to-face with a slim, white-haired creature about his age! She looked awfully tough too.

"So..." the creature said from beneath her cloak. "What do you have to say for yourself?"

Callum swallowed. The creature had on a sleek black-and-green suit that stretched from neck to ankle. The triangles of violet face paint under her eyes reminded Callum of dragon teeth. Callum had never seen a Moonshadow elf in person, but he was pretty sure he was standing in front of one—one that was holding two immense, gleaming silver blades inches from his face.

"You're...you're not who I thought you were," Callum stammered, slowly backing away from the blades.

The elf glared at Callum and removed her hood.

"That's far enough, human," she said. She lunged forward, sticking one of her blades toward Callum's chest. "If you just stay still and cooperate, I won't have to hurt you. I'm looking for someone in particular."

"Oh, is that so?" Callum said. His eyes darted to a couple of guards standing fifty yards behind her. They didn't appear to be looking in Callum's direction and he was reluctant to make any sudden movements. He tried to signal to them by raising his eyebrows wildly.

"What are you doing?" the elf asked.

"Nothing," Callum said. "I just, uh, don't want you to get hurt either."

"What in Xadia are you talking about?" the elf asked.

"Them!" Callum shouted and pointed to the guards, who finally took notice of the intruder. "Help!" he yelled. Then he turned and ran, leaving the elf behind.

Rayla whipped around and faced the guards, who were coming at her with their swords. But ill-prepared human guards were little more than a nuisance to Rayla. She ricocheted from wall to wall, swiping at the guards with her blades, then landed right between them.

The guards foolishly thought they had her cornered. As they lunged at her from either side, Rayla sprang up into the air. It worked perfectly—the guards slammed into each other and collapsed, unconscious.

Down the hall, Callum heard the crash of armor, then light

footsteps behind him. He raced up the stairway toward Viren's office. Lord Viren might not be his favorite person, but if anyone knew how to deal with this strange threat it would be him. With a bang, Callum burst through the doors.

"High Mage! I need your help," he shouted.

But the office was empty.

Moments later, the elf bumped Callum from behind and knocked him to the ground. He lost his grip on the scroll from King Harrow and it rolled underneath Viren's desk.

"What do you want from me?" Callum asked the elf.

"I'm an assassin," she said, looming over him. "But you don't have to die. That is, so long as you help me. I'm on a mission and there are only two targets tonight."

"Wait, two people have to die? What for?" Callum asked. There should at least be a rationale behind a killing.

"I'm the one asking the questions around here," the elf said. "I'm here for the evil king, and for his son—Prince Ezra."

"It's Prince *Ezran*," Callum responded impatiently, not really knowing why he felt the need to correct a stranger, much less an assassin. "But why? It's not fair. Why would you hurt someone who's done nothing wrong?"

The elf was undeterred. "Humans cut down the king of the dragons and destroyed his only egg, the Dragon Prince," she said. "Justice will not be denied. Your king and prince will pay for what the humans have done."

Callum's eyes filled with indignation. This was so wrong. Ezran would never harm an animal, much less the egg of one.

But this crazed elf clearly could not see reason. Callum knew there was only one way to protect his kid brother now. He looked the dangerous assassin in the eye and steeled himself. He needed to say each word with crisp clarity so the elf would believe his lie.

"I see. You found me. I am Prince Ezran."

Rayla paused. She hadn't expected such a ready admission. She'd always thought of humans as immense cowards. "You're awfully brave to tell me the truth, Prince Ezran. Awfully brave and awfully stupid." She raised her blades for the kill, for the deed that would earn back her place among the other assassins.

But she at least owed this young prince an explanation, right?

"I have to do this," she said. "I'm sorry. I don't actually want to, but I am duty bound."

"Why?" the prince protested. "Who is making you do this? You know this is wrong."

"An assassin doesn't decide right and wrong. Only life and death." Rayla parroted the mantra Runaan had so often repeated. She did not know if she was reciting the words to convince the prince that his fate was sealed, or to convince herself to seal it.

"That's very clever, but c'mon, really? How does this solve anything?" Callum asked. Though he was terrified for his life, he found himself strangely emboldened to argue with his would-be killer.

"This is justice. Humans attacked us unprovoked," the elf said.

"So, it's okay for you to do the same thing?" Callum prodded.

"Well, no, it's not the same thing," she said. "Because we are attacking you, provoked."

"Then it's a cycle," Callum said. "You hurt me, someone will get revenge against the elves. It won't end."

Callum felt his words had little effect on the elf; she practically embodied determination. He closed his eyes and prepared himself for the end. Would he feel pain? Or would it happen so fast that it would just be over, and then . . . nothing?

"Callum? Hey, Callum?" a high-pitched voice called out. It sounded like Ezran.

Callum opened one eye. There was a blade *very* close to his face, but he was pretty sure he was not dead yet.

"Callum!" The whisper was more urgent now and seemed to be coming from behind a large painting. Callum cursed his luck. This was exactly the wrong time for him to finally locate his brother, who was inside a wall, as usual.

"Go. Away," Callum said, trying to keep his lips from moving.

"I found something," Ezran continued.

"Are you talking to that painting?" the elf asked. She lowered her blades slightly.

"Uh, why would I do that?" Callum said. Then he faced the painting and loudly whispered, "It's not a good time."

"Is that because you're with a girl?" Ezran whispered back through the painting.

The elf clearly decided something was amiss. Keeping her eyes and her blades pointed at Callum, she went over to the painting, grabbed the thick golden frame, and gave it a yank.

Slowly, the painting swung open on a hidden hinge—it was a secret door!

Ezran was standing in the opening of a long, dark passage. He held Bait in one hand and a jelly tart in the other.

"Kid, get outta here," Callum yelled at his brother, still trying to bluff. He hoped Ezran would take the cue, sense the danger, and run before the elf could figure it out.

"Callum, what's going on?" Ezran asked.

Callum tensed. The young prince had always been too trusting.

"Callum? Who's Callum?" the elf asked. "I thought you were Prince Ezran," she said to Callum.

But Callum had barely opened his mouth when the elf's face turned a deep shade of purple.

"You lied to me!" she shouted.

"How is that worse than trying to kill someone?" Callum retorted.

Finally grasping the magnitude of the danger, Ezran gulped down the last of the jelly tart and held Bait out in front of him. He loved when his pet got a chance to use his secret weapon.

"Do your thing, buddy," he said to the toad.

Ezran closed his eyes—and hoped his brother did too— while Bait expelled a brilliant flash of light from his body. (While most of the time glow toads emitted a subtle mood lighting, the grumpy species had developed an intense flashing ability as a defense mechanism to blind would-be predators. The flash was usually used just as the predator's eyes grew widest with hunger.) The elf staggered backward, crying out in surprise.

"Callum," Ezran said when the light had faded. "Follow me. I have to show you something."

He pulled Callum into the dark passageway and slammed the painting shut behind them.

CHAPTER 7
CHANGE OF SOUL

Viren returned to his office gripping the basket stuffed with the useless snake—the incredibly rare, one-in-a-billion, magical, useless snake. If King Harrow had behaved according to plan, Viren would be amid one of his greater magical achievements—exploiting the twin-headed soulfang serpent to channel the king's soul into the body of another.

But no. King Harrow had selected today to develop a moral code. He had thrown safety to the wolves and there was nothing Viren could do about it. Claudia trailed behind Viren, questioning him incessantly. Her nonstop inquiries addled Viren, but he wore a mask of stoicism in front of his daughter.

"I don't understand," Claudia said. "The switching spell will save the king's life. Why would he say no?"

"King Harrow is a principled man," Viren responded evenly. It didn't matter that he agreed with Claudia; outwardly he would maintain a united front with King Harrow.

"You mean he's stubborn," Claudia said, with a roll of her flashing green eyes.

"Watch your tongue, young lady," Viren said. "But yes, he is hardheaded. Usually about the right things, but about this..." He trailed off.

"Are you worried, Dad?" Claudia asked.

Viren placed the wicker basket on his desk and leaned over it with a sigh. His intentions were good—he wanted to protect his king. But if the king rejected dark magic, Viren couldn't see a way out of this threat. He stared hard at the gold-framed painting hanging in the most prominent position in the room.

"You look so happy in that portrait," Claudia said, sensing her father's sadness.

In the painting, King Harrow and Viren stood side by side, young, strong, and hopeful. The king wore full armor and their faces were not yet lined with the stress of the recent years and war.

"I was happy," Viren said. "We posed for this painting a few days after King Harrow's coronation. He insisted I stand next to him for the painting. Because he knew I would stand by him through anything."

"And you have," Claudia said.

"So far, yes," Viren replied. As he stared at the painting, Viren remembered the man he used to be—a fiercely loyal and reverential high mage. So much had happened. But had he changed? Or was he still the same mage he saw in the painting? "I have to stand by him through this too. I need to be the man he once believed I was."

"What does that mean, Dad?" Claudia asked. Her father's face had hardened in the way it always did when he had made a final and important decision.

"It means, there's one more thing I can do to convince him," Viren said. "I have one last idea to save his life."

"That doesn't sound good, Dad. What, exactly, are you planning to do?"

"Claudia, if I told you, you would try to stop me."

"Doesn't that mean I should just try to stop you, then? Even without knowing . . ."

"Goodbye, Claudia," Viren said. He left the room, snake basket underneath one arm, and closed the door firmly.

The goodbye sounded unusually formal and final to Claudia. What was her father up to?

The slamming door had created a breeze, and something rustled on the floor near Claudia's feet. When she looked down, she saw a scroll had rolled out from underneath her father's desk.

She placed one dainty toe on the missive to stop its trajectory and bent down to examine the seal. It was King Harrow's: thick red wax imprinted with the two uneven castle towers.

Claudia picked up the scroll and placed it in one of the many hidden pockets in her gown, then looked around the office to see if anything else was out of place. A hideous painting her father kept of a gnarled shepherd and three adoring sheep protruded slightly from the wall. She examined the frame and noticed a sticky substance that looked remarkably like a handprint. She sniffed it. *Jelly.*

"Aha!" Claudia pulled on the painting's frame and it swung open. She peered into the depths of the dark passage.

Claudia snapped her fingers and a long bright ray of light sprang from her hand, illuminating the space before her. She started down the path.

"Hurry up, Callum," Ezran yelled.

Ezran and Bait were yards ahead of Callum, anticipating every twist and turn of the secret passage. Callum couldn't believe how adept his little brother was at navigating the dark passageways—Callum himself had never even laid eyes on them. The secret tunnels were cold and crypt-like. Loose stones and a strange dim lighting from glowing crystals made the winding paths even more chilling.

"What are these passages even for, Ez?" Callum panted as he tried to keep up.

"I'd love to tell you all about it, Callum, but maybe now is not the right time," Ezran said.

"Good point, let's keep moving," Callum said.

"Also, I have no idea about most of them," Ezran admitted.

The elf's voice called out from behind them. "You're only making this worse on yourselves!"

"I don't see how that could possibly be true," Callum replied.

"This way!" Ezran yelled. The two skidded to a stop in front of a stone wall.

"Oh no!" Callum said. "It's a dead end! What do we do now?"

But Ezran appeared shockingly nonchalant. "Relax, Callum. It's time for a puzzle." He gave Callum a quick smile. Then he turned back to the wall and started to tap out a pattern on some of the loose stones in the wall. After what seemed like forever, he stepped back.

"Wait for it," Ezran said.

A moment later, the floor beneath the boys began to grumble and creak. Callum realized the code had initiated some mechanism and now the stone floor was grinding apart, revealing a long spiral staircase to an even lower level!

The princes raced down the stairs, and at the bottom Ezran quickly dashed over to a small statue of a unicorn's head. He grabbed hold and turned it ninety degrees to the right, then pulled the horn down like a lever. The lever triggered the staircase to rise back up into the rocky ceiling. It shut with a loud *kerthunk*.

"You sure she can't follow us down here?" Callum asked.

"Positive," Ezran said with a cocky grin. He strutted across the room with his hands on his hips. "She'd have to press exactly the right combination of stones and rocks. It took me months to figure out that pattern. That elf would have to be Xadia's greatest brain genius to even have a chance of—"

But before Ezran could finish his sentence, the sound of rocks grinding resumed, and the staircase mechanism started up again. The elf appeared at the bottom of the stairs, unscathed and looking quite proud of herself.

"How—how—how did you figure it out?" Ezran asked. His arms had dropped to his sides in astonishment.

"Why don't you wipe that dazed look off your face," the elf said. "And while you're at it, you might want to wipe the jelly off your hands. Those sticky handprints showed me which rocks to press." She smiled a little.

Rayla walked toward the boys, her blades lowered now, taking in the secret room. Rickety wooden shelves lined the stone walls. The shelves were covered in dust and cobwebs and strange, unpleasant artifacts—animals preserved in jars, mysterious magic diagrams, live spiders with eerily pulsing abdomens in terrariums. Rayla looked in horror at bat wings pinned to the wall. It didn't help that the room smelled of mold.

"What is this place?" she said. "It's horrifying. Is that a diagram for butchering a baby deer? Who do these bones belong to? This place is disgusting."

Callum and Ezran followed the elf's eyes around the room. Both felt faintly ashamed at the sight, as if the elf had discovered a horror they themselves were responsible for.

Rayla glared in judgment. "Humans are terrible. Runaan was right. There's nothing in humans worth sparing. This place is a twisted abomination." Whatever small glimmer of empathy she'd developed for the boys had disappeared. "Time's up," she said, raising her blades once more. "Humans destroyed the egg of the Dragon Prince. There must be justice."

Callum jumped in front of Ezran. "You'll have to get through me if you want to hurt him."

"Really," the elf said. She did not look overly concerned. Callum might have been insulted in a different situation.

"Wait, please! You need to see something," Ezran said.

"I'm not falling for any more of your tricks, human," the elf said.

"There's no trick," Ezran said. "Look over here." He pointed to an oblong shape covered in a dusty white sheet. "I'll uncover it."

With one hand, Ezran quickly whipped the sheet away, like a magician performing his big reveal. Callum gasped. The elf seemed equally shocked.

A translucent egg as big as a human head shimmered and sparkled from the pedestal. Its iridescent blues and pinks and golds and greens lit up the terrible room with a soft, magical glow.

"It can't be," the elf said. She looked at Callum meaningfully.

"The egg of the Dragon Prince?" Callum said in awe. "So . . . it *wasn't* destroyed."

In the world above, the last light of day descended beneath the horizon. With the sunset, the crown guard escorted King Harrow across the courtyard and up to his defensive position high in his tower. Soon the moon would rise, and death would come.

CHAPTER 8
A LOUD MAGE

This changes everything," Rayla said, marveling at the egg's sheen and sparkle. Her anger had melted in the face of the beautiful object.

"So, this is it? The egg of the Dragon Prince? The cause of all this fighting between elves and humans?" Callum asked.

Rayla shook her head in disbelief. She had pledged herself as an assassin to avenge the egg's destruction, for while the death of the Dragon King was terrible, the Dragon King was grown and powerful and had committed questionable acts of his own. The egg was innocent. It was its destruction that had set the fires of anger and hatred in the hearts of Xadians.

"I can't believe it," Rayla said. "If the egg lives . . ."

"Maybe it could stop the war," Callum finished.

"Exactly." Rayla knelt close to the egg, gazing at its bright colors.

"It's doing okay," Ezran said. He ran his hand lightly over the shell. "I can feel it moving in there. I think it's healthy." He beamed.

"But I don't get it," Callum said. "Everyone believes the egg was destroyed. Why wasn't it?"

The question hung in the air, though no one expected the answer that came.

"Because my father saved it."

Rayla jumped at the raspy voice. There was a human standing at the bottom of the spiral staircase, glaring at her. She held a glowing crystal orb in one hand and appeared poised to cast a spell in the direction of the egg. Rayla's gentle kindness faded in an instant. She didn't hesitate to jump forward and draw her blades, blocking the human from the egg.

"Give me a break," Rayla said. "Your father didn't save the egg, he stole it."

"That's a lie," the human said. She leaned forward and her eyes narrowed. "And one little elf doesn't intimidate me. Callum, Ezran, get behind me. I can protect you." Claudia held her hand arched in the air, primed to draw a magical rune.

But Callum didn't move. He wasn't sure who to trust. Of course, he'd known Claudia forever and she'd never tried to harm him or Ezran. But it seemed that Claudia had been lying— or at least keeping a very important secret. On the other hand, the elf had admitted she was at the castle to kill Ezran.

Callum placed himself between Claudia and the elf. Ezran remained behind the elf.

"Claudia," Callum said. "If your dad didn't steal the egg, why is it here in his ... uh ... weird second office?"

"My father took it to protect us, Callum. So the elves and dragons couldn't use it." Claudia stepped closer to the egg as she spoke.

"What are you talking about?" the elf asked. She pointed a blade directly at Claudia's forehead. "How could we use it?"

"Don't play dumb. You know it's a powerful weapon," Claudia said impatiently.

"It's not a weapon. It's an egg!" the elf said, her voice rising to a shout. She seemed mortally offended at the idea of anyone exploiting the dragon egg.

But Claudia was done talking with the elf. They had nothing to learn from each other; her goal now was keeping the egg under human control. "Ezran, don't be afraid. Walk toward me, and if she moves even an inch..." Claudia began to draw a magical rune in the air. It was whitish blue and crackled and sparked with energy. A great tempest inside the primal stone surged, ready to release magical violence through the rune. "Just bring that thing here, Ez."

"It's not a thing," the elf interrupted. "It has a mother. And it needs to go back to her."

"You're right, it does want its mother," Ezran said, stroking the shell. Like this elf, he resented any animal being called a "thing."

"Ezran, please be careful," Claudia said.

Ezran looked at Claudia, who he'd known all his life. Then he looked at the elf, who was on a mission to kill him. But when he stroked the egg, he knew it was the stranger he should trust. This egg had to be returned to its mother. It was the right thing to do.

"Follow me!" Ezran said to the elf as he grabbed the egg. He turned and sprinted down a passage, away from Claudia. The elf didn't hesitate to run after him.

Should Callum follow? He still wasn't sure who to trust.

"Don't worry, Callum, I won't hit Ez," Claudia said. She looked as if she was preparing to unleash a powerful blast of magical energy.

Callum started toward the passageway.

"FOOL—" Claudia's voice was loud and commanding.

Callum paused. Had his supposed good friend just called him a fool for worrying about his own brother? That was it.

Callum raised his arm and knocked the primal stone out of Claudia's hand, then thought fast. He grabbed a rusted iron chain hanging from the ceiling and quickly snapped a manacle shut around Claudia's wrist. The chain wouldn't hold her forever, but it should at least give Ezran and the elf—and the egg—a head start.

"Callum, what are you doing?" Claudia pleaded. She looked at him like he'd lost his mind.

"The right thing, I hope," Callum said. Then he scooped up the primal stone off the floor and sprinted after Ezran and the elf, yelling, "I'm sorry, Claudia," as he ran.

"Uuugh!" Claudia let out an angry sigh that echoed in the

stone chamber. She couldn't believe Callum would betray her like this. He had always been such a sweet boy. Maybe he was just confused or under some spell cast by that elf.

No matter, though. Claudia's dark magic was as strong as any elf's primal magic. She would get out of this predicament and recapture the egg. She would make her father proud.

Claudia looked around the room for anything of use. She spotted a deep red, slightly melted candle within arm's reach. She knew it was a rare and powerful relic crafted from a dragon's earwax and the blood of a moon phoenix. The wick was something rare and unusual too, though she couldn't remember exactly why . . . But never mind that! A candle like this wasn't something to use lightly, but this was an emergency.

With a snap of her fingers Claudia lit the wick. On a nearby shelf she spotted a wooden container filled with the ashes of wolves who had died beneath a full moon, which she sprinkled onto the flaming candle. The flame turned a deep shade of purple and leaped at the air with magical potency. She held the candle up to her face.

Claudia muttered the cryptic words of the spell in a deep, throaty voice, and the whites of her eyes began to glow a purplish hue. She could feel the magic taking root in her body, twisting and turning through her organs. It began as a slow burn in the pit of her stomach, a throbbing, swelling bubble that rose into her head, taking over her eyes and breath.

At the final moment, she exhaled the magic over the flame and watched as the smoke and fire transformed into two shadowy wolves. The smoke animals took off down the passage at breakneck speed.

As soon as the wolves had fled the room, Claudia sank down to the floor, exhausted. It was the feeling she always had after dark magic, an aching void, a hollowness in her very soul. Her eyes faded to a deep, empty blackness. The wolves would do her bidding now, but each time she exploited these powers she felt it took her just a little bit longer to recover.

Callum hadn't yet caught up to Ezran and the elf, but he was getting closer. *Just a few more paces . . .*

Aaarrrooooooo.

A haunting howl rang out from behind Callum, then snarls.

Callum glanced back over his shoulder and saw something coming around the bend. Were those . . . wolves?

If so, they were unlike any Callum had ever seen, dark as the tunnel but somehow also glowing purple.

"There's something after us," Callum yelled. He could feel the hot breath of the beasts just feet behind him.

Rayla turned around to face the smoky threat and whipped out her blades. "Keep running," she said to the boys, ready to take a stand against whatever sorcery the human called Claudia had sent their way.

Ezran continued down a passage he knew would lead them to safety but then Callum took an unexpected turn.

"Wait, not that way," Ezran shouted.

Callum turned back to look at Ezran. "Why not?"

Thump! He ran directly into a wall.

"Because it's a dead end," Ezran said. He couldn't completely stifle a laugh, even with the impending danger.

Callum stood and rubbed his head. The elf was at the other end of the passageway battling the magical wolves. She jumped and flipped and soared through the air. She took perfect aim with her blades and drove both into one of the wolves' hearts.

But the wolf was unaffected. These were smoky, incorporeal shadows, and blades couldn't touch them. One wolf turned its head and bit down on the elf's arm. The bite sizzled, leaving black burn marks on her pale skin.

"This is useless," she said. "I can't stop them—they're just smoke. My swords pass right through." She stepped back toward the princes and looked around desperately for a way out. But they were all at a dead end together; there was nowhere to run.

Callum looked at the primal stone in his hand and remembered the spell he'd seen Claudia cast earlier that day in the courtyard. It seemed so long ago, when they sat together toying with Soren's hairdo using that wind-breath rune. The shape of the rune flashed in Callum's mind.

"There might be something I can do, but I don't know if I can do it," Callum said. What did they have to lose?

"Is this a guessing game?" the elf asked. Clearly, she had run out of patience. "Whatever you've got—just do it."

The wolves were growling with their heads down. They stamped their feet on the ground, preparing to make the final charge.

Callum tried to ignore them as he held the primal stone out in front of him and focused on its swirling interior. Then he traced out the angles and curves of the wind-breath rune, and to his surprise it seemed to be working—glowing lines and shapes appeared before him in the air, floating and shimmering.

Now, what was the word Claudia had said? Callum struggled for a moment to recall it and then it came to him.

"ASPIRO," he yelled, and blew the rune directly at the oncoming wolves.

A stiff, swirling whoosh of air emerged from his lips and enveloped the smoky predators. In a matter of seconds, they had disappeared into thin air. The tunnel was quiet.

"You did it, Callum!" Ezran exclaimed. He looked at his brother with new admiration. "You saved us."

"You never mentioned you were a mage," the elf said, sounding impressed. "This is an interesting turn of events."

"Who me? I'm not really anything." Callum shrugged.

"Um, you just did magic," Ezran pointed out.

"Yeah—that's what a mage is," the elf said. "A person who does magic. You're . . . a mage."

Callum couldn't believe his ears. After a lifetime of being terrible at just about everything he'd ever tried, Callum had done magic— and done it well. "Wow," he said. "I'm a mage! I'M A MAGE!"

"Shhhhhhh," the elf said. "Nobody likes a loud mage."

"Sorry, sorry," Callum said, lowering his voice. Then he whispered, with equal excitement but much less volume: "I'm a mage."

Callum, Ezran, and the elf breathed a little easier as they walked through the passages, though their relief was mild. They had survived the smoke wolves, but surely someone or something else would be after the egg soon enough. The elf stopped and looked hard at Ezran.

"Listen, I need you to give me the egg. I have to get it to the roof right away," she said.

"What? Why do I have to give it to you? I'm keeping it safe." Ezran pulled the egg a little closer to his chest.

"Would you just trust me?" she pleaded, reaching her arms out to relieve the prince of the egg.

"Heyyyy, sure," Callum interrupted. "That makes a lot of sense. We should totally trust you. Since we go way back... Remember that time like fifteen minutes ago when you chased me through the castle trying to stab me? Good times!"

Ezran gazed thoughtfully into the elf's eyes. "I want to trust you. But we don't even know your name."

"Assassins do not share their names," the elf balked. Then she sighed. "You may not realize it, but I'm trying to help you. Any minute now others will be arriving. Others like me. And they will not be so understanding. They are deadly and determined."

A look of understanding passed over the older prince's face. "Other assassins," he said.

"Yes, more assassins. Older and deadlier than I am—well, maybe not deadlier but definitely older. But they are only on a revenge mission. They believe that this egg was destroyed. If I can show the egg to my leader, I can stop them from making a terrible mistake. Just give it to me. Please."

But Ezran shook his head no. Although he believed the elf wanted to help, he didn't completely trust her yet.

"Ezran, if you want to live, you need to give me that egg now," the elf said.

"Hey, are you threatening him again?" Callum asked, starting to get angry.

"It's okay, guys," Ezran said. "I'm going to hold on to the egg, but I'll take you to the roof."

As Ezran led the way, the elf took a deep breath. "Rayla," she said. "My name is Rayla."

CHAPTER 9
VIREN'S SACRIFICE

Viren climbed the spiral staircase to King Harrow's bedroom, a look of quiet determination on his stony face. He held his staff in one hand and the wicker basket in the other. He didn't know if King Harrow had meant it when he said he'd rather lose his life than do this spell. But having decided to sacrifice himself, Viren felt a great sense of relief. Perhaps his life would serve a purpose.

The king's door was heavily guarded. Soren stood at the center, brandishing his sword in preparation for the assassins' arrival.

"So, what's in the basket, Dad?" Soren asked.

"Something that will protect the king when all your swords have failed," Viren said.

Soren looked at his father in confusion. "I'm not worried about my abilities, Dad, but you're not exactly inspiring confidence in the rest of the king's guard." The nearby soldiers were staring at the ground.

"Should they fail," Viren continued, "I am prepared to do anything to save the king. Absolutely anything. I hope you will understand." He hovered over Soren and gave him a weighty look. He did not expect Soren to comprehend now, but he hoped his son would remember these words later.

Soren stared back into his father's eyes but said nothing. Then he opened the door to King Harrow's room and let his father pass inside.

King Harrow sat slouched on his canopy bed, his gray robe spread out over the covers, his crown beside him. He held a small, framed painting in his hands.

"It doesn't seem like it was that long ago, but I felt so young then," King Harrow said, gazing at the painting. He hung his head mournfully. "I was young, and happy, and naive." He spoke the last words with more than a hint of bitterness. Then he waved Viren over to the bed.

"Ah, that old painting," Viren said with a smile. "A lovely young family. May I?" He reached out and King Harrow handed over the portrait. In the picture, a young King Harrow stood proudly next to his beautiful wife, Sarai. His arm was draped around her shoulders, and Sarai cradled baby Ezran in the crook of her elbow. Her other hand gripped the small hand of a very young Callum, who smiled broadly.

"The future I imagined for us . . ." King Harrow trailed off. "It was so much simpler than this. I thought I would be lucky enough to have a long, boring reign. I wish I could go back."

"Times were simpler," Viren agreed. "But you should know that as a father, you've had only successes. Those boys love and admire you. You did everything you could to help them through Sarai's death."

"I certainly tried," Harrow said. He'd brightened a bit at Viren's words, but then his shoulders slumped. "My life has run its course, and I deserve what's coming to me. But Callum and Ezran? Tonight, I'll leave those young boys without any parents. Who will guide them through that?"

"It doesn't have to be that way," Viren said softly.

King Harrow took the picture back from Viren. "What do you mean?" Then he saw that Viren had that basket beside him. His face flushed with anger.

"I've given thought to what you said earlier, My King," Viren said. He took a deep breath and prepared to make the ultimate offer. Saying the words was harder than he'd thought it would be.

"Oh, you've given it some thought, have you?" King Harrow asked. "Then why did you return with that abomination?"

"Yes, I've brought the soulfang," Viren said softly. "I have a proposal. Let me explain."

"Go on," King Harrow said.

Viren could tell the king's fuse was short tonight. Time was running out. And yet, he was having trouble being direct. He wanted simply to offer his life for Harrow's, but he wanted him to understand that this was more than just a sacrifice of a subject to his king. This was personal. "You are my king. But you are also my friend," he began.

"Your friend?" King Harrow asked, his eyebrows arched with suspicion.

"Yes, my friend," Viren said softly. He knew that over the years he had come to King Harrow with so many clever tricks and schemes, and he sensed that even now Harrow suspected an angle. Viren closed his eyes and took a deep breath. If he wanted the king to understand, he would need to be straightforward. He wanted to say simply *I love you* and *I will die for you*.

Viren looked the king directly in the eye. "Right now, I do not come to you as my king. I think of you as my brother." A strange euphoria swept through Viren as he spoke the words. A lifetime of ambition and struggle suddenly meant nothing compared to this moment of sacrifice and love.

But King Harrow wasn't having it.

"I see the problem now," King Harrow said. "It's that you believe you are special. Better than everyone else. Above the laws of this kingdom." With each word, Harrow's anger mounted. How dare Viren come to him in his final hours and lecture him about how they were equals. He pounded his fist against one of the bed posts.

"That's not what I am trying to communicate," Viren said. "Please, listen."

But there were too many worries swirling in King Harrow's

head. "Assassins are coming to murder me tonight and you're wasting what precious time I have left," he barked.

"No, Harrow—"

"Just stop," King Harrow said. He held up his hand to silence Viren. "In fact, if you're going to speak to me at all, you should address me correctly. How about 'No, Your Highness.' In fact, let's try 'Yes, Your Highness,' for a change."

Viren's face went white with rage. He'd come here with the best of intentions, prepared to give his life, and the king was too stubborn to even listen. He curled one lip up. "Oh, are you sure you wouldn't prefer 'Your Royal Highness'? Or 'Your Esteemed Inimitable Majesty' perhaps?" Harrow didn't deserve the loyalty Viren had been prepared to offer.

"I have tolerated your arrogance long enough," King Harrow said, standing. "Maybe even encouraged it. But if today is my last day as king, you will know your place."

"And where, exactly, is that place?" Viren demanded.

"Right here, on your knees," King Harrow commanded, pointing at the floor. "You are a servant of the kingdom of Katolis. You are a servant."

Silent, Viren bent to his knees.

He'd been stupid to even consider making this sacrifice. The king didn't consider him a brother or even a friend. In the king's eyes, he was worthless. He was nothing.

Viren's heart turned as cold as the stone beneath his knees. If he wanted to defy his former friend one last time, he'd have to do it tonight.

CHAPTER 10
RUNAAN'S MISTAKE

High above in the darkening sky, the moon was full, bright, and stunning. Rayla stood very still, alone atop the battlements. She closed her eyes and listened for her mentor's presence. Her sense of sight would do her no good tonight, for Runaan would undoubtedly employ the ability for which their kind was named—Moonshadow form. Under a full moon, the skill allowed a Moonshadow elf to shift their appearance so that it perfectly matched the light and shadow around them, rendering them completely invisible.

Rayla opened her eyes only when she was sure she heard a soft footfall. Clouds were drifting across the moon, leaving the battlements bathed in an eerie and gauzy glow.

"You're here. I know you are," she said. "I can sense your presence."

"Rayla," Runaan responded.

Even though she was expecting him, Runaan's deep, stern voice came as a surprise. He materialized as if out of the thin air and approached her slowly.

"Rayla, you defied me."

Rayla walked toward him, her hands up in a position of surrender but her voice urgent. "Runaan, you need to call off the mission," she said.

"You've lost your mind," Runaan said. He scoffed and shook his long white hair.

"Please listen to me," Rayla begged. "I've found something. The egg of the Dragon Prince!"

"That's impossible," Runaan said. He looked away from her.

"Instead of destroying the egg, the high mage stole it," Rayla continued. "He was going to use it for dark magic, but one of the human princes found it. The princes are trying to help me return it to its mom."

"Humans are liars. This is a trick and a trap," Runaan said. "You're a fool, Rayla."

Rayla opened her mouth to defend herself, but another voice beat her to it.

"She's not a fool," Callum said. He stepped out from behind the wall where Rayla had left him and Ezran hiding. This wasn't exactly *when* they had agreed he'd reveal himself, but there wasn't time to think about that. Rayla and Runaan turned toward him. "What she's telling you is true," Callum said.

"You've made a terrible mistake, human," Runaan said. He removed an arrow from his quiver.

"Ez!" Callum called out. "Show him . . . NOW."

Ezran stepped out and removed the blanket from the iridescent egg. It shone brightly in the dark night.

"It's . . . beautiful," Runaan said softly. He stood still, seemingly stunned by the majesty of the egg. He lowered his bow and arrow.

Rayla saw her chance. "Runaan, how can we take vengeance for an act that never happened? Now that you've seen this you have to call it off . . ."

Runaan paused for a long moment. Had Rayla gotten through to him?

But then he shook his head and held his wrist bindings out in front of him. "Rayla, you know it doesn't work that way. We bound ourselves. There's only one way to be released from this commitment."

"Runaan, please, that doesn't make any sense," Rayla pleaded. "There must be another way. This is a miracle and a chance for peace."

Runaan shook his head again. "The humans struck down the king of the dragons. Justice will not be denied. Now, give me the egg . . ." Runaan extended his hand and advanced toward Ezran.

Rayla knew that look in Runaan's eyes. It was no use arguing now. She drew her weapons and blocked him from the boys.

"Callum, Ezran—take the egg and go!" Rayla ordered.

"But—" Callum started to protest. It was just long enough for Runaan to shoot an arrow directly at him. He froze in fear.

But Rayla sprang into action. She unfurled her blades and smashed the arrow's shaft in midair.

"GO!" Rayla repeated. "Just keep that egg safe." Callum and Ezran scampered down the battlements. With them safe, Rayla turned all her concentration to Runaan, whose face was filled with fury. In an instant, Runaan disengaged a mechanism that split his weapon into two parts, transforming his great bow into two elegant blades.

The clouds seemed to take the elves' face-off as their cue and parted once again, revealing the full moon. Runaan began to transform, and Rayla followed suit. Their bodies became nearly transparent: translucent shadows outlined by a soft green glow. Rayla rarely used her Moonshadow form and found it somewhat disorienting, but she knew she could not allow Runaan even the slightest advantage. She raised her blades and took a deep breath.

"Don't do this, Rayla. I WILL kill you," Runaan said.

"Probably," Rayla replied, refusing to back down. Then she raced toward Runaan as he came at her.

Their weapons clashed in the air. Rayla went in for another swipe but Runaan beat her to it and she was forced into defensive mode. She blocked swipe after swipe.

"You're better than this, Rayla," Runaan said between swipes.

"No, not really. You've had about twenty years more training," Rayla said as she backflipped away from him.

"Not your fighting skills," Runaan said. "I mean your character." He delivered a hard blow to Rayla's torso. She blocked it but it sent her flying backward. Rayla decided to try using words as weapons one more time.

"You saw the egg, Runaan. There's no need for vengeance tonight."

All at once, Runaan stopped attacking. Rayla again wondered if she'd finally gotten through to him.

"You're just trying to stall me," Runaan said.

Okay, maybe not, Rayla thought. Time to change tactics. She leaned casually on one of her blades. "Interesting theory, Runaan. Care to discuss?"

Runaan glared at his young apprentice and folded his blades. "You laugh. But your behavior is treasonous." He shook his head. "I never believed you were doomed to turn out like your parents. But look at you. You've inherited their seed of weakness. Your justice will come later."

"I am not weak!" Rayla shouted, all humor gone from her voice. "How dare you accuse me of that? I'm nothing like them!" She angrily threw herself at him but it was too late. Runaan had turned away and leaped down to the courtyard.

Rayla seethed. Runaan hadn't killed her, but he'd stabbed her right where it hurt most.

CHAPTER 11
THE FELLOWSHIP
OF THE EGG

Callum, Ezran, and Bait left Rayla to battle her mentor and dashed down the stairs in search of a hiding place. In one corner of the deserted courtyard they saw an old wagon filled with hay.

"Over here, Ez," Callum said. "This should work." He hoisted Ezran and Bait into the wagon and covered them up as best he could. "You need to stay here—hidden. Keep the egg safe."

"Get in with us, Callum," Ezran said.

But Callum shook his head and looked up at the tower. "I'll go talk to the king. Tell him about the egg."

"Callum, why don't you just call him Dad?" Ezran asked.

Callum smiled. Ezran was always noticing little things, even when there were bigger—much bigger—things at stake.

"Because he's the king," Callum said, then paused. "And because I'm his stepson." He looked down at the ground.

"So what?" Ezran asked. "I think he would want you to call him Dad. I mean, if you wanted to."

"I don't know about that," Callum said. But he smiled at Ezran. "I'll think about it. Now, stay silent as a mouse and I'll be right back."

Ezran waited for Callum to get out of earshot. Then he looked over at Bait and said, "I've met more than one mouse who could create a racket if he felt like it."

Bait grumped in agreement. He hated when humans made assumptions about animals too.

Callum hurried up the spiraling stairs to the king's tower, brushing past a number of guards. But Soren intercepted him at the door to the king's chamber.

"Whoa, slow down there, Step-Prince. The king is pretty busy right now. Trying not to die and stuff," Soren said.

Callum was undeterred. "You're not stopping me, Soren." He reached for the door, but just then someone pushed it open from the inside. Viren emerged and Callum gasped—his eyes were the color of soot. Viren slammed the door behind him and glanced at Callum. His eyes faded to their normal steely gray.

"You should not be here," Viren said to Callum.

Callum looked around. Had anyone else seen the high mage's creepy eyes? This man had stolen the precious dragon egg—what dark magic had he been up to in the king's chambers? Callum was filled with a hot fury.

"I know what you did," Callum said. "You stole the egg of the Dragon Prince. We found it and we're keeping it safe."

"'We'?" Viren said with a mocking smile. "And just who, exactly, is this 'we'?"

"You think you're so intimidating," Callum shouted. "But the king will have you in shackles when he finds out about this."

"What makes you so sure he doesn't already know?" Viren said evenly. "Guards, grab him."

Callum panicked but Soren spoke up.

"But, Dad, he's the prince?" Soren said. Viren gave a fleeting dark look at his son, who immediately backed down and followed his father's orders.

"Do it!" Soren said. The guards obeyed.

Once the guards had restrained Callum, Viren slammed his staff on the floor. "Now tell me," he shouted, "where is the egg?"

Viren seemed to be losing his cool, and Callum decided that meant the king actually didn't know about the egg. He shook off all his fear of the high mage and looked him in the eye. "Let me go, or I'll call out to the king! I'll scream."

"Go ahead," Viren said. He had known *someone* would want to scream tonight, and he was ready for it. He reached into the leather pouch tied around his waist and removed a tiny black claw of a mummified cat. He folded it into his own fist and began to chant as his eyes turned purple. The claw began transforming into a putrid green mist.

Callum's eyes grew wide with fear. "Hel—" he began to yell, but he only got the first sound out. The green mist was now an ethereal claw. It swirled in the air toward Callum's open mouth, where it reached in and yanked his voice from his very body; a glowing ball of light appeared in the clutches of the phantom claw. The claw carried Callum's voice back to the mummified paw in Viren's fist.

Callum continued to yell but no sound came out. He gasped longer and harder to fill his lungs with air too. The look on his face was pure fear.

Viren felt back in control. "You impudent little mongrel," he snarled. "You were spoiled and given everything! And that has left you weak and helpless. Tonight, your world is changing and there is nothing you or anyone else can do about it." He squeezed his fist tighter, marveling at how effective his simple trick was.

Just then, a howling wind blew through the staircase, deep and strange and oddly warm. One by one, the sconces and torches fizzled out, leaving the entire tower in sudden darkness.

Soren shivered. "They're here," he announced. "Defend the doors."

He went to move into position, but a loud *whoosh* whipped down the corridor. Soren pushed Callum aside without a thought, taking his place, and not half a second later, an arrow stuck in his shoulder plate. Callum stared at Soren with unbelieving eyes.

"Oh, quit it," Soren said. "Just doing my job, Step-Prince."

More arrows suddenly flew from all directions, and shadowy assassins jumped from wall to ceiling. Not that Soren could see much—the elves were nearly invisible in the darkness. How many were there? They seemed to move like spirits and with the speed and freedom of the wind itself. Soren's heavy armor suddenly felt awkward. Still, he and the other soldiers did their best, swinging and blocking against the barely visible attackers.

Callum tried calling out, but his voice was still trapped in Viren's strange spell. Finally, in the confusion, a guard bumped Viren's hand and the enchanted claw fell to the floor. Callum's voice surged back into his chest.

"King Harrow!" Callum shouted toward the king's door. But by now, the entrance was blocked by a flurry of guards and elves. The shadowy figures were killing off the soldiers one by one. The bodies were piling up, each having given their life for the king.

For Callum's father.

"DAAAADDD!" Callum called out.

But there was no response. The only sounds were the clashing swords and the cries of the wounded.

Then Callum heard a small voice in the distance.

"Callllluuuum. Calllluuum. Where are you?" It was Ezran.

Callum glanced out a tower window and saw Ezran in the courtyard searching for him. But how could he leave the tower when the king was in so much danger?

Callum tried to think of what the king would want him to do.

"I'm coming, Ez," he called out the window.

He gave one final look back at the door to King Harrow's chamber, then bolted to the spiral staircase. He took the stairs two at a time, trying not to look at the dead bodies strewn on the way to his little brother.

"Callum! Did you talk with Dad?" Ezran asked, when Callum was safely in the courtyard. They were hugging tightly.

Completely out of breath, Callum just shook his head no.

Out of nowhere, the elf—named Rayla, Callum now knew—leaped down from a wall. She looked at the boys and confessed, "I couldn't stop him."

Callum nodded. "I know. I just came from the tower."

Rayla's eyes filled with concern. "Say the word and I'll go back into that tower with you," she said. It seemed a genuine offer to take sides against her own, to defend what was right.

Callum gazed at the tower where chaos and bedlam ruled. Then he looked back at Ezran with his wide, innocent eyes and his arms clutching the egg. Everything felt suddenly quiet. Suddenly clear.

"No. It's up to us now," Callum said. "We must return this egg. We have to keep it safe and carry it to Xadia."

"And find its mother," Ezran added.

"If we return this egg, we could change things," Rayla said. "We could actually make a difference."

"Just the three of us," Callum said.

An unpleasant, grumpy snort interrupted the bonding

moment. Bait was staring at Callum, his usually yellow skin flushed a deep, angry red.

"I meant the four of us," Callum corrected, and Bait returned to his usual golden hue. "Come on, let's go."

They scrambled out of the courtyard, slipping through the castle gates. On the castle bridge leading to the forest, Ezran suddenly stopped.

"Callum, do you think Dad will be okay?" Ezran asked as they turned back to look at the tower one last time.

Callum didn't want to lie to Ezran, but he didn't want to distress him even further. After a long pause, he said, "Our dad has the finest guards in the kingdom defending him."

"Yeah, that's true," Ezran said, sounding relieved. "Yeah, of course things will be okay."

Rayla gave Callum a look. Certainly, the finest guards were defending King Harrow. But both of them knew that might not make a bit of difference.

Under the full moon, the brave women and men of the Katolis crown guard fought valiantly to protect their king. Many laid down their lives. But when the battle faded as nighttime ebbed, the balcony doors of the king's tower opened. A wounded survivor stumbled outside and collapsed onto his knees. One of the white bindings on his wrist turned a deep shade of crimson, as if it were magically soaked in blood. It loosened and fell to the ground.

With his last bits of strength, Runaan secured the blood ribbon to the arrow crafted by Ethari, its head carved in the shape of a bird of prey. He tightened the knot, and the jeweled eye of the bird suddenly shone as if alive.

"Regina draconis," he called out as he released the arrow. It flew off into the sky, sprouting red, smoky wings. The arrow would carry the message of the king's death across the continent, to the queen of the dragons.

Just moments later, a handful of remaining human guards led by Soren apprehended Runaan on the balcony. Runaan dropped his weapons, closed his eyes, and placed his hands at his sides, palms facing forward. He was ready to receive his destiny.

"Finish this," he said without remorse.

"My pleasure," Soren said and raised his sword high above his head.

"No, wait!" Claudia shouted. She placed her hand between Soren's blade and Runaan's neck. "We can find more practical uses for this one. Tie him up."

CHAPTER 12
A SLEEPLESS NIGHT

Callum, Ezran, and Rayla (and Bait) walked silently through the forest. Callum thought this may have been the longest day of his life. It had started out like any other, with sketching and parrying. Now, he roamed the woods with Ezran and an elf, trying to save a dragon egg that the entire world believed had been destroyed. Nothing would ever be the same.

While Callum was lost in silence, Rayla noticed one of her bindings loosen. The pearl-white ribbon turned bloodred and then slipped off her wrist. She stared at the magical binding in awe and then instinctively, looked skyward. A bold, strong shadowhawk flapped its wings in the sky above, red smoke trailing its path. Rayla stifled a gasp.

Ezran and Callum turned around at the noise.

"What's going on?" Callum asked. "Is something wrong?"

Rayla wondered if Callum could see in her eyes that yes, everything was wrong. Despite the miracle of the egg, an unnecessary and painful tragedy had unfolded.

Rayla collected herself. Her human companions had suffered a life-changing loss, but it wasn't her job to tell them their father died. "We should stop and rest," she said instead. She stopped at a large flat rock and sat down. "It's a long journey to Xadia. This is as good a place as any to rest for the night."

The princes looked at each other, then back at Rayla, their faces full of surprise.

"What, you don't think we're going to make it to Xadia in a single evening, do you?" she asked.

"It's not that . . ." Callum said. "It's just, we've never slept in the woods before—we don't really know how."

"Oh, right," Rayla said. *Princes.* She would have a little fun with this. "It's real easy. You just take whatever it is you are carrying and use it as a pillow and blankets. You humans do sleep with pillows and blankets, don't you?"

Callum gave her a look that said he didn't appreciate her sarcasm, but he and Ezran bunched up their sacks into pillow-shaped lumps and wrapped themselves in their cloaks anyway. They laid down on the hard ground. Rayla watched from her rock.

"Hey, what about you? Aren't you going to sleep?" Callum asked.

"In a little while—I'm still wide awake," Rayla said.

Callum knew how she felt. How would he ever fall asleep given all that had happened in the past few hours? Terrifying visions of the battle he'd witnessed flashed in his mind as the forest wind whipped over his face. The pebbles and sticks poking into his back weren't making matters any easier either. But the emotional toll of the day had exhausted him more than he knew; in an instant, he was asleep.

A few feet away, Ezran lay on the ground looking enviously at his sleeping brother. He gathered Bait up in his cloak and closed his eyes. He imagined he was back in his bedroom, the crackling fire nearby and the cool, feathery pillow against his cheek. He envisioned every detail in his mind. Now his father was opening the door, coming in to sing him to sleep. Ezran breathed in deeply and hummed the lullaby to himself.

"The Sun is down, and the Moon is high.
Baby yawns wide with a sleepy sigh.
The Sky fills up with Stars that blink.
Baby's eyelids start to sink.
The Ocean kisses the Earth good night.
The waves say hushhh . . . little babe, sleep tight."

Somehow, Ezran felt as if his father were there with him. He was almost sure he could feel the king's warm lips press against his forehead. And as usual, he yawned and was off to sleep.

Nearby, Rayla's heart skipped a beat. She knew that melody— her mother used to sing it to her when she was a wee elf. She gazed over at the sleeping prince, so innocent, so peaceful. In that moment, she knew she wouldn't follow through with Ezran's assassination.

The binding on her wrist suddenly tightened ... or at least Rayla thought it did. Was it her imagination? Just a guilt-ridden conscience manifesting itself in physical torment? Whatever the cause, it was time to get this binding off.

She stood up and rubbed the ribbon against some rough bark, but the ribbon held fast. She gnawed on it, pulling so hard she thought her teeth might come out. Nothing. The ribbon just snapped back into place.

Rayla looked up from her wrist and locked eyes with Bait, who was also awake. In fact, he was giving her a cool, hard stare. As if a glow toad was capable of suspicion.

"What are you looking at?" Rayla whispered at Bait. "Don't you know what I'm risking by doing this?"

What the glow toad—and the princes—didn't know was how dangerous it was for humans and an elf to travel together. And surely there would be search parties looking for the missing boys.

Rayla lay back down on her rock, but her mind was still too full of worries about the journey to let her sleep.

Even if they made it to Xadia alive and well, what were the chances Callum and Ezran would be accepted? Even Runaan, who had seen the dragon egg firsthand, had continued on his path of vengeance.

Rayla yanked on the assassin's binding around her wrist once more. Would *she* be welcome back in Xadia, having teamed up with the very person she had been bound to kill?

She laughed to herself. She didn't know what was more ridiculous: that she had teamed up with a human prince—no, *two* human princes—or that Runaan, the person she trusted most in the world, had tried to kill her tonight.

He hadn't, though, in the end. That thought was comforting, at least.

Rayla looked at her other wrist, the naked one. Her mentor had completed his mission. Had he survived while doing so?

Bells tolled in the distance, interrupting Rayla's train of thought. The sound could only mean one thing—the announcement of the king's death to the citizens of Katolis.

Rayla rolled over, away from the princes. She would tell them about their father, but not yet.

Right now, the only thing that mattered was getting that egg back to its mother.

CHAPTER 13
VALLEY OF GRAVES

The bells tolled in a ceremonious rhythm for King Harrow's pre-dawn funeral procession. Viren led the march through the streets of Katolis, walking slowly and deliberately as bleary-eyed citizens emerged from their homes to take in the news of their king's demise. Word spread quickly and soon the citizens surrounded the procession holding candles, some crying softly while others looked on in silence. Dour pallbearers carried King Harrow's casket, careful not to disturb the wreath of red roses draped atop.

Opeli, the high cleric of Katolis, followed closely behind Viren. She carried an ornate torch for the ceremony at the funeral pyre. Her long blond hair and youth belied a scowl that covered her entire face.

"A funeral so soon is madness," she hissed at Viren's neck. "Our people have always mourned fallen monarchs for seven sunsets. You've not even given him one."

"I understand your concern, Opeli," Viren replied smoothly without turning around. "But in a time of crisis and war, we must move forward. We cannot have the citizens of this kingdom wallowing in despair when so much is at stake."

"Time to grieve is not the same as wallowing," Opeli said, her eyebrows furrowed. "Our traditions give comfort and closure. Rushing the process is wrong, Viren."

"The only thing that matters now is closure," Viren replied, ending the conversation.

They led the procession through the entire lower borough, down into a deep canyon. Royalty had been buried at the Valley of Graves for generations, but not every king or queen earned a place. Enormous statues carved from rocks towered over the line of people.

Soren and Claudia walked alongside each other past the crypts and monuments. This wasn't the first time they'd seen the Valley of Graves, and it was never anything less than awesome. Soren stretched his arms over his head and stifled a yawn—the fighting had only ended a couple of hours before.

Beside him, Claudia looked concerned. "Keep your head up, Soren. This is important," she whispered.

"I know—it's been a really long night," he said.

"Here, take this," Claudia said. She removed a flask from her cloak and poured some steaming potion into the top. She handed it to her brother, who eyed it skeptically.

"What, exactly, are you trying to get me to drink?" he asked.

"I call it 'hot brown morning potion,'" Claudia said with a smile.

Soren took a dainty swig from the cup and his eyes widened with delight. He swallowed the rest in a single gulp.

"That is delicious, Claudia!" he said. "And it revived me almost instantly." He shivered a little. "Pour me another."

Claudia refilled the cup and Soren drank again, this time more thoughtfully.

"Not only does it give me energy, the flavor is just right. Do I detect notes of stone fruit? There's definitely some floral flavors in there." Soren looked up from his beverage to see Claudia staring back at him as if he had been speaking an unknown Xadian tongue. "What? I've got a refined palate."

"Hmmm—if you say so," Claudia said. She took a sip and shrugged. "I just detect notes of hot and brown."

The procession continued, finally coming to a halt at the funeral platform. Under Viren's orders, soldiers had worked quickly in the night to erect the funeral pyre in the center of the valley. The sky was beginning to brighten with the first light of morning as the clerics mounted the stone steps and the pallbearers lay the king's body down. Then the clerics took their places at the four corners of the platform. The flag of Katolis flapped lightly in the morning breeze. Viren walked to the front of the crowd, leaned on his staff, and addressed the mourners.

"Today we woke to a devastating truth: Our king has been taken from us. Slain by the forces of Xadia—vile Moonshadow elves!"

Murmurs and gasps echoed throughout the valley, just as Viren knew they would. He put a hand over his heart and continued.

"To me, Harrow was more than a king, more than our greatest warrior. During his final hours, I was deeply moved when Harrow called me his brother." He paused for dramatic effect. "It is with a heavy heart that today we lay him to rest. High Cleric—it is time to light the pyre."

He turned to Opeli and nodded, but the high cleric didn't move.

"We cannot do this now," Opeli said. She held her torch steady. "Where are the princes? They should be here for their father's funeral."

Viren had known Opeli would bring that up. He regretted the response he was about to give, though it did help his cause. Since the princes were last seen with the single escaping elf, he could assume only one thing. He looked at the expectant crowd, then closed his eyes and hung his head. "There is no nice way to say this, so I will say it simply. The princes are dead."

The crowd gasped. To kill a king was awful enough, but innocent children? The princes' deaths could put the kingdom in a state of chaos. Who would rule now? Who would succeed King Harrow?

Viren had suspected this information would roil the people.

A strong leader would be a relief to them now. It didn't matter who that leader was, as long as he brought a sense of certainty and security to the fearful mobs.

"Now do you understand, Opeli?" Viren shouted. "Now do you see why we cannot let our enemy's cruelty go unanswered, why we must move forward with strength?" His nostrils flared with impatient indignation, and he commanded her this time. "Light the pyre!"

But once again, the high cleric disobeyed. She slammed her torch on the platform to extinguish the flame. The other torchbearers followed her lead until they all stood in darkness.

Viren watched each flame fizzle out. Opeli may have proven that she had a few followers, but he was still in command of this ceremony. He turned to Claudia.

"You know what to do," he said.

Claudia nodded at her father and uncorked a small glass jar she'd been carrying in her pocket. A rare emberback spider frantically scampered out, the flame-like pattern on its abdomen glaring in the early morning light. She let it scuttle across her fingers for a moment, staring at it dotingly as if it were a pet.

But the second the emberback reached her palm, Claudia squelched it. The dead creature's orange blood seeped through her fingers.

"Semalf gnippiks gnipael," Claudia chanted slowly as the goo dripped down her hand.

Her eyes glowed with purple energy, and she slowly unfurled her fingers. Golden red flames shot up from her palm, arcing toward the kindling of the closest brazier on the platform. The fire took hold and magically leaped from brazier to brazier and finally toward the altar. It circled King Harrow's body like a buzzard homing in on its prey and then plummeted to the pyre. A moment later, the massive blaze enveloped the king.

Opeli, the torchbearers, and the citizens watched in horror as King Harrow's casket turned to smoke and ashes. In minutes, the only remnants of the king were dark plumes drifting skyward.

Viren looked at his daughter with satisfaction. Then he stood in front of the altar, the fiery blaze dancing behind his head like a crown of flames.

"When a ruler of Katolis dies, we mourn for seven days. But we are at war. Today we must mourn sevenfold, for tomorrow—there will be a coronation."

CHAPTER 14
SAD PRINCE

Callum woke on the forest floor with his palms sweating and his heart palpitating in his chest. It wasn't a dream—he had run away from home with a Moonshadow elf. And not just any elf, an assassin who'd broken into the castle to murder his little brother. What had he been thinking?

Callum watched Rayla in the early morning light through half-open eyes. She was sitting on the same rock she'd been sitting on last night, sharpening her blades. Did elves not need sleep? Had she been sharpening those things for hours? They looked sharp enough to split a piece of thread.

Callum couldn't see Ezran but he could hear his brother's slow and steady breathing nearby. If the elf would just go for a walk or get distracted somehow, he could wake Ezran and they could make a run for it. Go home. Find safety somewhere else.

Then a bright bluish glow caught Callum's eye—the dragon egg poking out of Ezran's backpack.

Callum sighed. They couldn't return to the castle with that. If there was even the slightest chance that this elf could help them return the egg to the Dragon Queen, Callum should find a way to work with her.

"Do humans always sleep this late? Or are princes just particularly lazy?" the elf said, breaking Callum's train of thought.

"Uh, I don't know," Callum said. There was a gnawing pain in his stomach where food should have been. He pulled his knees up to his chest, afraid his stomach would growl. He couldn't show weakness, needed to stay strong.

GROWWWWWLLLL.

Callum rolled his eyes. Had Rayla heard?

"Is your stomach trying to impersonate your grumpy glow friend?" she asked.

Bait glared at Rayla and grumbled.

"I haven't eaten for a long time," Callum said.

"Yeah—I'm feeling a few hunger pangs myself," Rayla said. "Why don't I go try to find us some food?"

"That's really nice of you," Callum said. "I'm happy to help." He started to get up, but Rayla waved him off.

"You'll be just as much help staying out of the way for now," she said. "Besides, it's traditional for mages to steer clear of anything dangerous, such as gathering fruits and berries. I'll be back!" And she scampered off.

Callum shrugged, still glad just to be called a mage, even if it meant extra teasing. He was glad to get some alone time too. He pulled his sketchbook out of his backpack and started drawing, letting his pencil lead. He had found that sometimes, when he had a lot on his mind, sketching helped release the thoughts and worries. He let his hand make lines and curves on the page, not even thinking about what he was drawing. Maybe a quarter of an hour later, a voice startled him.

"I'm back," Rayla said.

Callum looked up. He'd been so focused on his drawing he hadn't even noticed her looming over him. This foggy-brained behavior was not good. He had to be more aware of his surroundings. He shook his head has he looked back down at his drawing. Oh no! He'd been drawing the elf! He quickly turned the page.

"So, what have you got there?" Callum asked.

Rayla held out a small picnic of fruits and berries.

"I'm not going to lie to you, Callum," she said. "We have better fruit in Xadia. The selection over here is bit meager." She knelt and lay out the fruit. "But I was pleasantly surprised that you do have moonberries on this side of the world." She pointed to a bunch of bloodred berries.

"Moonberries?" Callum looked at the bunch skeptically. "Those look a lot like the berries we call death berries. Known to have the rather unpleasant side effect of certain death."

"Well, Wise Mage, it turns out you are correct, but I am also right. Moonberries come from the exact same bush as your death berries and look identical in the daylight. But under the light of the moon, the ones that glow are moonberries. Not only are they not poisonous, they are super nutritious, delicious—even medicinal. One berry is enough to keep you full for nearly an entire day."

"Wow. So, they look identical, but they might kill you or they might save you," Callum said.

"Exactly. Just like me . . ." Rayla smiled.

Callum's eyes widened. Was she joking?

"Humor is a thing you have on this side of the continent, right?" Rayla teased.

"Ha." Callum forced an awkward laugh.

"Anyway, don't touch them for now, we'll sort them tonight and separate certain death from tasty treats," Rayla said.

"Don't worry," Callum said. He ignored his growling stomach and turned back to his sketch pad. He decided to draw something a bit safer this time, the stone from Claudia. He pulled it out of his bag, sketched out a circle, added a few forking jags of lightning, and then went to work shading the swirling clouds.

"Hey, what's that you're drawing over there?" Rayla leaned over Callum's shoulder. "You're a talented artist."

"Oh, not really," Callum said. "I just . . . I draw. It's what I do. I draw when I'm stressed, I draw when I'm happy. Right now, I'm just trying to draw this . . . primal ball."

"Primal stone," Rayla corrected.

"Right," Callum said. "It holds the pure essence of a primal spirit inside."

"Primal source," Rayla said.

"Right."

"You do know what the six primal sources are?" Rayla asked smugly.

"If I say yes, are you going to make me name them?" Callum asked. He was growing a little weary of this game.

Rayla motioned for Callum to hand over the sketchbook, which he did—cautiously.

"All magic in the world comes from the six primal sources," Rayla began. "They're the original and purest forms of magical energy." She drew six runes on the page, one for each primal source. "The Sun, the Moon, the Stars, the Earth, the Ocean, and—?"

Callum looked at her blankly and Rayla tapped the stone in his hand.

"Oh! The Sky," he said.

"Yes. To cast a spell, a mage needs primal energy. So that wind-breath spell you did? You'd usually need a storm, or at least a strong breeze. But with that stone, you have all the power of the Sky anywhere, anytime."

"Wow," Callum said. He couldn't believe his luck.

"Primal stones are incredibly rare," Rayla said. "They've been sought after by the most powerful archmages in history. And now . . . somehow you have one." She raised one eyebrow and handed Callum back his sketchbook.

Callum studied Rayla's rune drawings for a minute. Something looked familiar . . .

"Wait! I've seen these before," he said. "At the Banther Lodge, our family's winter home. These symbols were carved into this little . . . cube thing. What if that cube is magic? We have to go get it!" He grabbed his sketchbook and jumped up.

"Whoa, slow down," Rayla said. "We have bigger things to worry about. Dragon egg, ending a war, remember all that?"

"Xadia's to the east, right? So is the lodge," Callum said, putting his sketchbook in his bag. "Isn't that lucky? We can stop on the way."

"Sounds great," Rayla said. "I'm sure the lodge won't be crawling with humans. Humans who are looking for you and who want to kill me. Yay!"

Callum stared back at her, confused.

"That was the humor again," Rayla said.

"Oh." Callum blushed. "Well, there won't be anyone there. It's the winter lodge. It's been empty for months. Trust me."

Rayla stared at Callum with her arms crossed.

Callum sighed. He'd have to plead his case harder. He couldn't believe he was about to admit all this to an elf, but he figured he didn't have much to lose.

"Look . . . Rayla," he said, feeling the still unfamiliar name on his lips. "Princes are supposed to be good at things. Sword fighting, leadership, riding horses. But I've always been kind of bad at . . . well, everything."

Rayla dropped her hands to her sides. "I'm listening."

"So, when I tried that spell, I thought for sure I'd end up on fire, or covered in spiders—but it worked. And when you called me a mage, I thought ... maybe that's what I'm supposed to be. So, if this cube thing could help me learn more about magic, I—" Callum stopped. Rayla had an odd look on her face. Maybe spilling his life story wasn't the best idea after all.

Nearby, Ezran stirred, and Callum jumped at the opportunity to move on. He knelt next to his brother.

"Hey, Callum, I had a weird dream," Ezran said as he sat up. His hair was a tangle of twigs and leaves.

"It wasn't a dream, Ez," Callum said gently. "All of that was real."

"Are you sure?" Ezran asked. "There was this giant pink hippopotamus, and I pulled its ears off. Because it was made of taffy."

"Uh ... no, that was a dream," Callum said. "But the elves, the dragon egg, the smoke wolves ... that was all real."

"Then I tried to thank the hippo for the taffy," Ezran continued. "But it couldn't hear me, because I was eating its ears!"

Callum shook his head. His little brother was clever and imaginative even in his dreams.

"Hey, sad prince," Rayla interrupted. "Let's go get your cube." She had pulled on her cloak and looked ready for a mission.

"Really?" Callum asked.

"Yes. Just please no more detours, all right? Or heartfelt speeches."

Callum beamed. Then he grabbed Ezran by the shoulders and looked at the dragon egg between them.

"Ready to take this little guy back to his mom?" he asked Ezran.

"Yeah." Ezran smiled.

Callum gave Ezran a final squeeze, took a deep breath, and glanced back at the castle. It would probably be a very long time before he saw his home again—if he ever did.

CHAPTER 15
AUNT AMAYA

Hours later, Callum and Ezran trudged behind Rayla, trying to keep up with her pace. Callum wiped sweat from his brow, and Ezran paused to rest his head on the egg.

"I'm tired," Ezran said.

"No breaks," Rayla responded. "Especially not when we're on a human-led detour."

"But I'm really hungry," Ezran said.

"No snacks," Rayla said. She didn't even turn around.

"I'm thirsty," Ezran whined.

"No drin— Wait, actually, I may have something for that." Rayla pulled a small glass vial from her belt. The bottle was filled to the brim with red liquid. Rayla held it out toward Ezran. "Drink it," she said.

"Oh, that's okay," Ezran said. "Actually, I'm not that thirsty."

"Seriously? I don't believe you," Rayla said. "You've been complaining all day."

"It's just that we don't drink that . . ." Callum said, pointing to the crimson liquid. He was trying his best to be polite and respectful of other cultures.

"Drink what?" Rayla asked.

"You know . . ." Callum whispered the last word. ". . . blood." He looked away. "We don't mean to be rude, but, uh, you can keep it. The blood, I mean."

Rayla stared at Callum. "It's juice." She handed the bottle to Ezran, still holding Callum's eye. Ezran sniffed the vial and then took a sip.

"Is that what humans think we are? Bloodthirsty monsters?" Rayla asked.

"Wait . . . is that moonberry juice?" Callum asked. He felt a hot blush creep from the bottom of his neck to the top of his forehead. Why did he keep embarrassing himself in front of her?

"You learn fast," Rayla said. Then her voice brightened. "What do you think of the juice?" she asked Ezran.

Ezran took another big slurp. "It's refreshing, filling, energizing . . . and tangy!"

Rayla laughed and grabbed the vial back before Ezran could finish the whole thing off, and began walking again. "You thought elves drink blood. How ridiculous! I suppose we all got brought up being taught scary things about each other. I mean, I always heard you scary humans eat the flesh of animals. Crazy, right?" She laughed.

Behind her, Callum and Ezran exchanged a look. Callum raised a finger to his lips, and Ezran suppressed an awkward smile.

☽

"Finally! We made it," Ezran said. He pointed through a thicket to the enormous hunting cabin tucked near a wide river. The cabin was a two-story wooden A-frame structure. It looked odd this time of year with windows boarded up and the roof missing about a foot of pure white snow. A small fishing boat bobbed in the water near a tiny dock.

Callum felt a little spark in his step now that they were so close, but Rayla grabbed his elbow and held him back.

"What is it?" Callum asked. "See? No winter, no humans at the winter lodge."

"I still don't feel good about this, so let's make it quick," Rayla said. "You both wait here. Just tell me where the cube thing is, and I'll be in and out."

"Fine," Callum said. "Let me at least draw you a picture so you'll know where to find it." He pulled out his sketchbook and made a quick drawing of one of the upstairs rooms. "This is a bedroom," he said, pointing to a window on the second floor. "From that room, walk into the hall, go past the suit of armor, then the game room is the first door on your left. The cube should be in there, packed away in a toy chest." He tore the picture out of his book and gave it to Rayla.

"I'll be quick as lightning," Rayla reassured Callum. She dashed off to the cabin with the drawing clutched in her hand. Callum and Ezran stood just inside the tree line.

"You know what's weird?" Ezran asked.

"What?" Callum responded. He was watching Rayla swing herself up to the second floor and pry open a window.

"That there's no one here, since this is where we were supposed to go last night. Where Dad told us to go."

Callum grimaced. How had he not thought of that? "You're right, Ez. We probably shouldn't have come here. But she'll be fast. We'll be out of here before you can say—"

A bugle sounded in the distance, followed by the pounding thumps of galloping horses. A group of soldiers were making their approach.

"Come on!" Callum shouted. "We have to get inside and warn her before they see us!"

They raced toward the front door of the lodge, but when they got there, it wouldn't budge. They turned around to face the approaching troops.

A legion of three dozen horses came to a halt directly in front of them. One rider, heavily armored and radiating confidence, dismounted. This was clearly the leader. An ornate helmet covered the warrior's head. Callum gulped as the soldier put one enormous hand on the helmet and removed it.

"Aunt Amaya?" Ezran asked. Callum's eyes went wide.

Aunt Amaya shook out her cropped, jet-black hair and brushed it from her face, revealing a long scar on her cheek. Amaya was the princes' mother's sister. She was a great general and a fearless leader, known across the land for her brilliant battlefield strategy and improvisation. And more important (as far as her nephews were concerned), she was known as one of the greatest breakfast chefs of all time.

She swept the boys into a bone-crushing bear hug and lifted them off the ground. But Aunt Amaya didn't say anything to Ezran or Callum—she had been born deaf and signed to communicate.

Commander Gren, Aunt Amaya'a assistant and interpreter, dismounted and quickly ran up beside her. Gren was young, freckled, and a little awkward, but his sign language skills were impeccable. He stood up straight and got close to Amaya so he could see her hands.

"I'm so glad you're safe," she signed, once she'd let go of the boys. "You are safe, right?" Gren repeated the words out loud.

"Extremely safe!" Callum said, probably a little too forcefully. "Safe and alone." He thought about Rayla searching for the stupid cube and filled up with guilt.

"Glad to hear it," Aunt Amaya signed, but she gave him a weird look. "I received an urgent message from your father and I came as soon as—" Aunt Amaya stopped mid-sign. She scanned the front of the hunting lodge.

"That's odd—I thought I saw something. Did any of you hear anything?" she signed.

Callum and Ezran exchanged a nervous glance.

"You mean like, a sound?" Ezran asked. "Because, then . . . no."

Gren quickly translated, but Amaya ignored Ezran and marched to the front door. Callum tried to intercede.

"Oh, that door is locked," Callum said. "You wait here for a minute, and I'll go find the spare key."

Amaya lifted Callum from underneath his armpits and put him to the side. With one swift move, she kicked the enormous double doors. They ripped from their hinges and crashed flat in front of her, spreading dust and soot in their wake.

"I don't believe in locks," she signed, and proceeded inside to the foyer.

The boys followed steps behind. Everything seemed to be in place. Hunting trophies mounted the walls, lush green and gold rugs covered the wooden floorboards, and the long staircase leading to the second floor looked just as it had in the winter.

Out of the corner of his eye, Callum saw Rayla's shadow high up on the rafters. He prayed his aunt had been looking in another direction. She was standing perfectly still; only her eyes moved, flickering around the room.

"Someone's here," she signed.

"Whaaaat? No. It must be some disturbance caused by one of your HUMAN TROOPS!" Callum shouted toward the ceiling, not so subtly trying to warn Rayla.

"It looks like you're shouting," Amaya signed to Callum. "You know it doesn't help to yell. I'm completely deaf, remember? And why are you saying, 'human troops' like that?"

"What do you mean?" Callum signed back to Amaya; he'd learned quite a bit of signing over the years. "That's how I always speak when I say, 'HEAVILY ARMED HUMAN TROOPS.'" There Rayla was, leaning against a slanted rafter, looking furious. Callum knew he had to think quickly. He grabbed his little brother and shoved him in front of their aunt.

"Aunt Amaya!" he said and knocked on her armor to get her attention.

Amaya looked down at Ezran, and Rayla seized the opportunity to leap to another rafter just out of sight.

"Ezran has something to tell you," Callum said, hoping his brother might be able to come up with a suitable distraction faster than he could.

"Ummmmmm," Ezran stalled. "I skipped breakfast. I'm sorry."

Aunt Amaya frowned. As a breakfast connoisseur, she was offended that Ezran would neglect a hearty morning meal. Amaya had traveled the world and mastered breakfast tricks everywhere she had been. She could make muffins better than any baker in Duren and poach eggs with syrupy golden yolks like the farmers in Del Bar. When people skipped breakfast, Aunt Amaya took it as a personal affront.

"Breakfast is the most important meal of the day!" she signed. "You two, march yourselves into the dining hall and take a seat at the big table. NOW!"

As they marched toward the dining hall, Callum saw Rayla swing from another rafter and land lightly on the second-floor hallway. "Well played with breakfast," Callum whispered to Ezran.

Callum looked at his hands nervously while Aunt Amaya rooted around in the pantry, opening cabinets and drawers, pulling out kitchenware and generally creating a ruckus. When she burst into the dining room she was holding several loaves of bread and wearing a wide grin. Gren followed quickly behind her.

"Well, the bad news is this bread is so stale...that it's weapons-grade," Amaya signed. She slammed a loaf on the table so hard the princes jumped. Amaya laughed.

"So, what's the good news?" Ezran asked.

"The staler the bread, the greater the victory when I achieve my perfect recipe for Aunt Amaya's Lost Bread," she signed. "Gren, go secure the ingredients from the travel rations. You know what I need."

"Of course, eggs, milk, salt and—" Gren said.

But before he could continue Amaya raised her hand to stop him.

"Oh, right. I almost said your secret ingredient out loud," Gren said. "I'll be more careful."

When Gren left, Amaya sat down with the boys and started signing. Callum translated for Ezran.

"Aunt Amaya says she received a message from our dad yesterday," Callum said. For the first time in twenty-four hours, he remembered the letter King Harrow had given him in the throne room. He felt around for the scroll in his pocket—but it was gone. Callum swallowed hard. King Harrow made such a big deal out of giving him the letter and somehow, he had lost it.

"What's wrong?" Amaya signed.

Callum shook his head. "Nothing," he signed.

Amaya looked dubious but she passed Callum the letter she'd received, and signaled for him to read it aloud.

"'General—the castle is under threat. Assassins have infiltrated the kingdom. Moonshadow elves.'"

At "Moonshadow elves," Callum looked up—Aunt Amaya was scowling and shaking her head.

"They're the worst kind," she signed.

"'Do not bring your forces to the castle,'" Callum continued. "'Though I know you will think I am crazy, your orders are to proceed immediately to the Banther Lodge. Callum and Ezran will be there. Above all, see to it that my sons are safe.'" Callum put down the letter. It felt good that the king had called him his son.

"And so, that's why I'm here," she signed. "To ensure your safety. Why don't you two go upstairs and play while I work on breakfast."

Half an hour later, the boys could smell sweet sugary deliciousness wafting up from the kitchen into their bedroom.

"I can't wait for this meal," Ezran said. "But I think after we eat, we should tell Aunt Amaya about everything. About the dragon egg and Rayla."

Callum shook his head. "She'll never understand, Ez. Elves and humans do not get along, and that's not going to change because some kids think it should. I mean, look at the toy you're playing with."

Ezran glanced down at the figurine in his hand. It was an elf—but it wasn't. It looked nothing like Rayla. Its horns were disproportionately large and its four-fingered hands were oddly twisted. There was an angry grin on its face. The toy was monstrous.

Ezran sighed. Maybe Callum was right. But he could hardly think straight right now, he was so hungry.

"Lost Bread for Lost Princes! Come and get it!" Gren called up from below.

Ezran and Callum bolted down the stairs, grinning as they passed Aunt Amaya, who was on her way up.

Meanwhile, Rayla moved through the lodge, successfully dodging the many human troops investigating the building. Once the game room had been searched and marked clear, she slid into it silent as a cat, and closed the door behind her.

Rayla consulted Callum's drawing, which was remarkably realistic. Not a thing was out of place.

"Well, it's not bad," Rayla said to herself. *Getting the cube should be easy enough with this drawing, now that I've eluded those idiot guards.*

She found the small treasure chest Callum had mentioned and emptied its contents onto a table. A bunch of old keys fell out . . . and a cube with a different rune on each side.

"Huh," Rayla said. She had never seen anything quite like the cube. But before she could examine it, she felt a warm breath on her neck. She turned around just as a huge shield came crashing down on top of her.

Rayla's training kicked in and she backflipped away from her attacker. She barely had time to whip out her blades though; the soldier—it was that general who seemed to be related to the princes—came running at her with the enormous shield again.

Rayla defended herself against blow after blow, hardly believing the warrior was handling that heavy, cumbersome weapon with such grace. The shield was so solid it made Rayla's butterfly blades look like playthings. And the general's reflexes were quicker than she thought humans' were supposed to be. So fast, in fact, that she knocked one of Rayla's blades from her hand.

Shocked to be left with a single weapon, Rayla did the only thing she could think of—she ran. The general followed, smashing furniture and columns in her pursuit of Rayla. A moment later though, the soldier stopped in the middle of the room. Was she surrendering?

Amaya stood motionless in the center of the game room. She'd had enough of this wisp of an elf. She held her shield in one arm, and with the other hand beckoned the elf to come attack her.

The elf took the bait. With a running start, she leaped up into the air and descended on Amaya. Amaya easily blocked her and sent her flying against a wall, where she pinned her. She drew her sword, prepared to vanquish the assassin. But as she steadied herself for the kill, Amaya caught a change in the light. Someone had entered the room behind her. Keeping the elf pinned to the wall, Amaya turned around to see Gren.

"General Amaya, the princes have disappeared," Gren signed, a look of panic on his face.

Amaya glared at the elf. It was one thing to attack a king, but these monsters were attacking innocent children. If Moonshadow elves had kidnapped Callum and Ezran, it might be better to keep this elf alive for the time being. She backhanded the elf with her heavy gauntlet, and the elf went limp.

CHAPTER 16
A MONSTROUS LIE

R ayla's pounding headache was matched only by the hollow ache in her jaw. She opened her eyes and regained focus; she was in a dark basement with the general called Amaya looming over her and two guards nearby. The guards were holding her confiscated blades. Rayla twisted and struggled, but her wrists were tied with ropes.

"How did you do it?" Amaya signed. Gren stood beside her, translating her signals into common tongue for the elf.

Rayla thought quickly. "How did we do what?"

Amaya's eyes narrowed. "'We'? How many of you are there?"

Rayla suppressed a small, sly smile. She thought her trick might just work after all. "Did I say 'we'? It's just me. I'm alone."

Amaya tensed as if she might strike Rayla again, but at the last minute, she stood upright.

"Liar," she signed to Rayla. She turned to the guards. "If there are more of them, the princes are in danger. Do not take your eyes off her." Then she left the room.

Rayla watched the guards watch her. One of them examined Rayla's confiscated blades, trying to figure out how they worked. Rayla barely suppressed a laugh as the guard accidentally jerked the mechanism, flipping one of the blades open and startling himself.

"Careful with those," Rayla said. "Wouldn't want to lose a finger. I mean, can you imagine going through life with only four fingers?" The guard stared back blankly. "Get it? Because . . ." She wriggled her four-fingered hands.

Just then, a screeching sound came from the wall across the room. Both Rayla and the guards turned to see an old dumbwaiter descending down an open shaft. It was moving at an agonizingly slow speed, so slow that the guards seemed mesmerized by it. Rayla squinted in the dim light, trying to get a better look at what was on the platform.

Finally, finally, the full platform came into view.

It was Bait!

He gave Rayla a meaningful look and she realized that a plan had been hatched for her escape! The guards weren't so quick to follow. They blinked at the strange creature.

"Have you met Bait?" Rayla asked the guards. "He has a special talent. He may not look that smart, but he's actually very bright."

Slightly offended but taking his cue, Bait flashed his brightest glow and blinded the guards. They staggered around, shouting and swinging their weapons. Rayla took the opportunity to angle the ropes binding her hands toward their wildly swinging weapons.

"A little to the left," she said as she maneuvered the ropes into the path of one of the swords.

Snap! The ropes broke and Rayla was free.

"Thanks!" she said. Then she tripped the guards, snatched back her blades, and sprinted up the stairs. Halfway up she stopped though. That grumpy glow toad had saved her life; the least she could do was save his. She dashed back into the room and scooped him up just as Callum and Ezran came tumbling from around a corner. She shoved Bait into Ezran's hands and ran past them.

"Come on, they're distracted, we've got to get out of here now," she yelled.

The three of them ran through the lodge and out the front door, soldiers in pursuit.

Rayla was surprised to see it was nighttime outside. How long had she been unconscious?

"This way! To the river," Callum yelled, running toward a bridge. But just as they reached the bridge, three soldiers appeared on the other side. Callum turned every which way looking for an escape route, but they were surrounded by Aunt Amaya's troops.

"Stop right there, elf," Gren yelled, translating Amaya's orders. "Callum, Ezran, come here."

But the boys didn't move. Aunt Amaya looked at them quizzically.

"Callum. We should tell her," Ezran whispered.

"Boys. Don't make me say it again," Aunt Amaya signed. "Get away from her."

Callum didn't know what to do, but the choice was his to make. He looked from his brother to Rayla, then followed her gaze to Amaya. The elf and human were staring each other down, their eyes full of hatred. He suddenly had an idea.

"We can't move, Aunt Amaya," Callum said while he signed. "She'll kill us if you come any closer! She said if anyone tries to stop her, she'd drink our blood!" Callum did his best to ignore the hurt on Rayla's face as he spoke. "She's a Moonshadow elf! She's a monster!"

Callum's idea seemed to be working. The soldiers looked terrified, and even Aunt Amaya lowered her weapon. Callum widened his eyes at Rayla, silently begging her to play along. She refused to return his gaze but seemed to take the hint.

"That's right, humans," Rayla said. "I dare you to take another step. I haven't tasted blood in days."

"See? It's too dangerous," Callum said. "She told us if you let us leave, she'll abandon us safely in the woods tomorrow. So, it's best for everyone if you just go."

"Don't be fooled, Callum," Aunt Amaya signed. "Elves are liars and she won't keep her word. There's only one way to deal with this type." She turned to Rayla. "You know what that is, elf."

Then Amaya turned to her bowmen, who stood poised and ready. "Do it, take the shot."

As commanded, the bowmen loosed their arrows, which raced straight for Rayla's head.

Still reeling from Callum's words, Rayla was slower than usual but still managed to unfurl a blade and deflect one arrow. She turned to dodge the other, but it caught her braid, severing the white plait and pinning it to a tree several yards away.

Rayla put her hand to her head where the braid had been. A hot fury boiled up inside her.

"Go ahead, take another shot. But the next time I swing my blade, I'll end both these boys in half a second." Rayla's heart was pounding but she locked eyes with Amaya and grabbed the princes by their shoulders, as if they really were hostages.

There was a long pause. As the seconds ticked by, fear, hurt, and anger raged inside of Rayla. Even she didn't know what she'd do if further provoked.

"Stand down," Amaya finally signed to her troops. They lowered their weapons.

"Move, humans," Rayla shouted. She poked Callum in the back with her blade, and the boys started walking. "What now?" she hissed at Callum.

Callum led them out of sight of the soldiers to the fishing boat docked at the river's edge and shook off Rayla's grip. He and Ezran (and Bait) climbed in.

But Rayla lingered at the edge of the water, watching the boat rock side to side with the boys' weight. She didn't like where this plan was going.

"Uh, I don't think a boat—" she started.

"Just get in!" Callum whispered.

Gren's voice shouted Amaya's stern warning from the distance. "If you lay a hand on those boys, I will hunt you and the rest of your wretched kind to the ends of Xadia!"

Rayla glared at Callum but stepped into the boat and cut it free with her blade. The strong current grabbed hold of them and swept them down the river.

Callum looked back at the Banther Lodge and exhaled a long sigh of relief.

"That worked! I can't believe it," he said.

"I can't believe you're such a jerk," Rayla said.

"What?" Callum was confused. "Rayla, stop. What's wrong?"

But Rayla wouldn't look at him.

"Leave me alone," she said. Her voice wobbled a little and she turned away from Callum.

"I don't understand," Callum said.

Rayla spun around. "Of course you don't. You have no idea how it feels to be called a monster. Or looked at like you're some kind of animal."

Oh. Callum got it now.

"I didn't mean any of it!" he said. "Aunt Amaya's the one who hates elves. I was just using that against her."

"Well, it worked. Now every one of those humans is even more convinced that all those stories of horrible bloodsucking elves are true."

"I'm sorry," Callum said. "I just didn't think about it that way." The words had saved Rayla's life, hadn't they?

Rayla sighed, apparently done with the conversation. She dug into her pocket, and when she pulled out her hand, she was holding the rune-etched cube.

"You found it!" Callum said. A little spark ignited in his belly.

"It's a toy," Rayla said. "Probably a die from a children's game. I hope it was worth it."

She tossed it to him then hunkered down where she was sitting in the boat.

Callum felt like he might burst. He plopped down near Ezran and rolled the cube on the floor of the boat a few times. He wasn't sure what he was hoping for, maybe that his newfound mage-ness would unlock some secret power of the cube or something.

But the cube remained unchanged, and the spark in Callum's belly lessened. Had he risked everyone's life for a silly toy?

Frustrated, he tossed the cube to the side. It landed near Bait and suddenly one side flickered with a pale, yellow light.

Callum dove for the cube and grabbed it, but the light dimmed and went out. *Huh.*

He paused for a moment. Maybe the primal stone could help. He reached into his cloak and withdrew it, then held the cube up to the sphere. The cube's Sky rune glowed a bright blue. *Interesting!*

Callum pulled the objects away from each other. The cube stopped glowing.

That spark inside Callum's belly grew again. He didn't know what the cube was or exactly what it could do, but he had every intention of finding out.

Amaya and Gren watched the boat as it disappeared down the river.

"Don't worry, Amaya," Gren signed. "We'll follow them. We can catch them if—"

"No," Amaya signed. "If the elf realizes we've followed them, she'll take the princes' lives. I have another plan."

"Very good," Gren said.

Amaya turned to the soldiers and signed as Gren translated. "Corvus!" A cloaked man with a stern expression emerged from the gathered troops. He was tall and muscular but stepped lightly. "I trust your expertise in this," Amaya signed. "Track the princes, but stay out of sight. And when you see an opportunity, free them."

Corvus nodded, his dark eyes glinting. This was the type of mission he relished. "I won't lose them," he said with utmost confidence.

Amaya nodded and turned back to her troops. "The rest of you—ride with me."

CHAPTER 17
RITUAL AND
CORONATION

It was the second dawn since King Harrow's death, and the sun ascended the mountaintops as it always had. Despite the fact that he'd barely slept these past two days, Viren felt fresh and rested. The kingdom was headed in the right direction for the first time in a long time.

But one look in the mirror and Viren felt defeated all over again. Years of dark magic had taken a toll. The darkened circles around his eyes were now permanent, and his face was marked with lines of stress and aging: deathly pale skin, unnatural dark spots and streaks, and creases so deep that "wrinkles" couldn't describe them.

Some of the effects had occurred gradually over time, while others had come on suddenly after unusual or especially potent spells. Viren accepted these changes as a cosmetic side effect of an important tool. But other people were not so understanding. He had learned that his true appearance was both shocking and terrifying.

He double-checked the lock on his study door and then opened a nearby cabinet. A panel slid away to reveal a secret enclosure, a glass terrarium filled with butterflies in every color of the rainbow. The insects flapped their delicate wings, flitting back and forth in search of some escape.

"Good morning, little ones," Viren cooed.

The butterflies were sunray monarchs he had captured near the border of Xadia. He'd been breeding the creatures for years.

Viren opened the screen and placed one weathered hand inside the terrarium. A single butterfly landed on his forefinger, flapping its vibrant purple-and-yellow wings. He used his other hand to stroke the delicate wings.

Every time he enacted this ritual, Viren was reminded of the first time he had performed it. He remembered his relief when it worked, restoring his appearance. He remembered how he'd been filled with hope, certainty even, that this would change everything. He remembered hurrying home, ready to be forgiven. And even more clearly, he remembered the bitter hole left in his soul when Lissa told him his restored appearance changed nothing. Even though dark magic had helped their family, saving their son's life—she seemed to fear him and hate him now, and he knew he could never repair that.

Viren shook the memories away and performed the spell. The

rings under his eyes faded and the gray in his hair turned black. His cheeks became rosy.

He took a deep, satisfied breath, then exited the study. He closed the door behind him, leaving a colorless, lifeless butterfly on the floor.

Viren strode down the hallway to King Harrow's chambers. Today was the day he had barely dared to dream about. And yet, somewhere deep down he had always believed it would happen; King Harrow had manifested weaknesses that Viren was immune to.

King Harrow's room was still scarred from the battle the night before last. The curtains were shredded, and the furniture was overturned. The only living reminder of Harrow was his songbird, Pip, sitting silently in its golden cage. Viren walked over to a large mirror, which had the coronation robes laid out nearby. Across the room, Claudia was standing by the door leading to the balcony.

"Are you sure about this, Dad?" Claudia asked. She glanced at the crowds gathering below the castle.

"Quite," Viren said without taking his eyes off the mirror. "Claudia, I will take the crown humbly, because I wish to serve. Who else can help in this time of great need?"

"But do you think the people are ready to accept this transition of power?" Claudia said. "We still don't know what happened to Prince Ezran and Prince—"

"They're dead," Viren said quickly. He knew Claudia was close with the boys, Callum especially, but he'd already told her this news multiple times.

"It can't be . . ." Claudia said.

Viren softened. "I'm sad too, Claudia. But it's the only logical conclusion I can come to. You know how dangerous and deadly the elves are—how could those boys have survived?"

"But, Dad, that elf seemed different from the rest. She was being nice to the princes—it was almost as if they had joined her side. Maybe somehow, they are still alive and she's protecting them."

Viren had been over this with his daughter too. "Your optimism is charming, Claudia, but not exactly realistic. Your friends are no longer alive." He paused. "Sometimes tragedy can give birth to new beginnings," he said. "The best hope now is to find strength and unity and move the kingdom forward. We want the people to let go of the painful past and look forward to a brighter future." Viren smiled at his daughter, and Claudia nodded in response.

"Now, help me with these robes, my dear."

Claudia approached her father, and a few attendants scurried over to drape Viren in the coronation robes. They worked methodically, fingers straining to fasten buttons and lace sleeves. Viren appreciated their efficiency, but by the time they placed the last layer of robes on Viren's shoulders, a strange tension had seized the room. The attendants seemed to be murmuring among themselves. Viren tried to ignore it—he didn't have time for silly gossip today—but he eventually lost his patience.

"What is it?" he yelled. "What are you idiots all whispering about?"

No one dared answer, but a few pairs of eyes flicked over to the songbird. Pip was staring at Viren—glaring even. A slow smile crept over Viren's face.

"Oh," he said, turning to face the bird and patting down his robes. "No song for the occasion?"

Pip remained still and silent.

Wasn't expecting one, Viren thought to himself with a smirk. Then he stepped through the curtains and onto the balcony.

An enormous crowd had gathered in the courtyard below. The early morning air was crisp and cold, and Viren shivered despite his many clothes. Guards flanked the crowd, bearing weapons and torches. And there was Opeli, waiting for him on the balcony, with the crown in her hands. Viren ignored the cold expression on her face and addressed the crowd.

"People of Katolis. King Harrow's death has wounded us deeply, but the loss of his sons—our princes—is a greater injustice. By eliminating both heirs to the throne, our enemies sought to leave us without a leader."

The crowd was silent. Viren could practically see their anxiety.

"It would disgrace Harrow's memory to allow the kingdom he loved to be lost in darkness," Viren continued. "Though it is a heavy burden, I will humbly take up the battle in Harrow's name. I will become Lord Protector of the realm."

The crowd gasped and Viren knelt. Slowly, with her hands trembling, Opeli reached out to place the crown on Viren's head. He closed his eyes in anticipation, but the crown did not come.

Get on with it! he silently urged the high cleric. She would soon learn the consequences of all this disobedience. One second passed. Two. Viren's senses heightened—there was a murmur in the crowd, which quickly turned to a commotion. His eyes sprang open when he heard a voice he recognized all too well.

"Stop the coronation," Gren shouted for General Amaya, who was signing rapidly. "The princes are alive."

Opeli retracted the crown and backed away from Viren, a small smile on her face.

"Finish!" Viren commanded desperately, remaining on his knees. But she shook her head.

Viren's face flushed with humiliation. He was not one to forget such an indignity.

CHAPTER 18
A SHOCKING TURN

Rayla woke up to her hand throbbing. She repositioned herself and opened her eyes. Early morning light streamed through the trees of their camp. A few feet away, Callum was lost in concentration, examining the rune cube. He held it up to the primal stone, and a bright light shone from the cube, then faded when he pulled the cube away. Then shone when he held it to the stone, then faded when he pulled it away. Over and over. He'd hardly put that thing down since they left the lodge.

Behind Callum, the little boat they'd arrived in was bobbing up and down in the water. Rayla closed her eyes again—anything to forget about that boat. And besides, she wasn't ready to start her day with the princes. It turned out humans were exhausting.

A few minutes later, a bright light shone very near her face. Then dimmed, then shone again. Over and over.

"This doesn't end well for you," she said. She pushed Callum's hand away and opened her eyes.

The cube rolled over to Bait and the side facing him glowed yellow, illuminating his grumpy face. Rayla sat up as Callum retrieved the cube.

"Last night you thought the cube was just a worthless toy," Callum said. "But now we know—"

"That it's a glow toy?" Rayla teased.

"Exactly!" Callum said.

"Exactly," Rayla repeated, still not convinced the detour to the lodge had been worth it. She stood up and her hand throbbed again. *Uh-oh.* "I'm going to find us some food," she said.

When Rayla was certain she'd distanced herself from the princes, she scrambled up a pile of rocks and examined her binding. There was no question about it now—the binding was getting tighter. She massaged her wrist in an attempt to keep the blood flowing.

"Time to get this thing off," she said.

She unfurled her blades. Handcrafted and sharpened by the elf Ethari, the blades were guaranteed to slice right through the flimsy ribbon. Carefully, making sure the blade avoided her skin, Rayla slipped it under the ribbon.

"Easy now," she whispered to herself.

With a single, swift movement, Rayla jerked the blade upward. The ribbon held fast.

She moved the blade back and forth like a saw but found she couldn't make even the smallest tear in the ribbon.

"What is this thing made of?" she said to no one.

"Heeellllllp!"

Rayla's ears perked up at the call of distress. It was coming from their camp.

"Help! Helllllllpp!"

That was Callum's voice! Rayla grabbed her blades and sprinted back to camp, leapfrogging from tree to tree. She arrived with her blades ready for action.

"What is it? What happened?" she asked. Her eyes darted back and forth in search of the threat, but Ezran and Callum were alone in the clearing. Callum was holding the primal stone in one hand. His other hand crackled with a powerful electric current. Beads of sweat poured down his forehead as static electricity sparked all around him.

"Help!" Callum yelled.

Rayla rolled her eyes and folded up her blades. Callum was in a magical predicament, but nobody's life was in danger.

"He tried to copy this spell Claudia did, but he doesn't know how to finish it," Ezran said from behind a rock.

"Yeah, I only saw her do the first half," Callum stammered. "But I'm very good at the first half."

"Seriously?" Rayla said. "That sounds like a really good and safe idea."

"Lecture well deserved," Callum said. "But let's focus on the future. What do I do now?"

Rayla scratched her head. "When you release a spell, there's usually a word or a phrase or something in ancient Draconic . . ."

"Well, I don't speak dragon," Callum said, some exasperation creeping into his voice. "Does anyone around here speak dragon?"

"You didn't hear Claudia say anything?" Rayla asked.

"I think she might have called me a fool when I interrupted her doing the spell?" Callum replied.

"Well, she might have been right about that," Rayla said. "Give me a second. I know some Draconic words, just let me think . . ." She closed her eyes in concentration.

"You know what," Callum said a moment later, "don't worry about the Draconic words . . . I'm just going to throw the stone."

Rayla opened her eyes. "What? No, don't do that."

"Yeah, I'm going to throw you the primal stone," Callum said.

"Sounds like a good plan," Ezran piped up from behind his rock.

"NO, that is not a good plan," Rayla said. She waved her hands wildly in the air. "Throwing the primal stone is bad."

"I won't throw it; I'll just gently toss it," Callum said.

"No, no, no! No throwing, no tossing," Rayla said. Why could humans not understand that magic was not a plaything?

"Tossing it . . ." Callum insisted. He leaned back and lobbed the primal stone into the air toward Rayla. Immediately, the spell energy dissipated and Callum fell backward.

Rayla caught the orb . . . and suddenly wished she hadn't. Her hair stuck straight up, buzzing with static.

"Phew," Callum said. "It worked. I'm okay now."

"You're kind of making a sizzling sound," Ezran said to Rayla. Rayla glared at Ezran.

"Sorry about that," Callum said. "I guess I'm just so excited to be learning magic, I got a little carried away." He shrugged his shoulders.

Rayla gently dropped the primal stone, and her hair settled down into its natural state. "Okay. Enough almost killing me," she said. "The sooner we return this egg, the sooner maybe this war can end. It's time to hit the road." She bent down and tossed the primal stone back to Callum, then walked toward the woods.

Callum put the primal stone safely back in his bag. That could have turned out a lot worse—not that he'd admit that to Rayla. But where was she going?

"Road?" Callum said. "Why wear ourselves out walking on a road, when we can let the river do the walking?" He pointed to the boat. Then Callum waggled his eyebrows up and down a few times, thinking that would really sell the idea.

"Nope." Rayla shook her head. "Say goodbye to the boat. We go by land from here."

"But why? The river's going the right direction and moves much faster than we could ever go on foot. I mean, look at those legs." Callum pointed at Ezran's stumpy legs.

"What? I have nice legs," Ezran said. He examined his calves.

"We're walking, and that's final," Rayla said.

Callum thought Rayla was being awfully pushy about no boat. "Is there maybe another reason you don't want to take the boat? Something you're not telling us?" he asked.

"No. There's absolutely no secret reason," Rayla said, overcompensating a bit.

"So, wait. Let me get this straight," Callum said. "Are you like this fierce, backflipping, tree-climbing, sword-stabbing elven warrior . . . but scared of a little splish-splashing?"

"Awwww. That's cute," Ezran said.

"Oh please," Rayla said. "Fine, we'll take the dumb boat!" She stomped over to the boat and climbed in. Then she sat on the bench with her arms crossed over her chest. "Let's go."

Viren paced up and down the throne room. He'd agreed to a meeting with Opeli and Amaya, and now the king's sister-in-law was rattling off commands as if she owned the place. Gren tried to keep up.

"We must establish order, that's what the people need—a plan. And the top part of that plan is finding the princes," Amaya signed.

"Your strength makes me calm," Opeli said to Amaya. "And your presence will reassure the people in the wake of this tragedy and crisis."

Viren scowled. Opeli was *really* getting on his nerves. "I quite disagree. Amaya is creating confusion, allowing uncertainty to rule the day. Missing princes? An empty throne? Katolis will be paralyzed. I was prepared to return a sense of certainty to the people."

"You're going to solve this, Viren?" Amaya signed. "You are

the one who let things come to this. The king's death happened on your watch."

"You speak as if I invited these assassins," Viren said.

"I left our stronghold at the Breach—have you any idea the dangerous forces gathered at our border?"

"I'm well aware," Viren said. That's why they needed a leader ready to take action.

"We rushed back here, but you had already failed," Amaya signed.

Viren seethed. It was embarrassing to have to defend himself like this. "I did everything in my power to protect King Harrow—I was willing to give my own life!" he said. His eyes smarted with tears.

"Then what went wrong, Viren? Why are you the one still here?" Amaya asked.

"Harrow went wrong," Viren said. How could Amaya not see this? She was no stranger to their willful king. "His own stubborn ways stopped me from helping him. You know him as well as I do; his pride was more important to him than his life."

Amaya considered this. Then she looked from the empty throne to Viren in his coronation robes. "You wanted this outcome," she signed.

Viren's eyes went wide. "How dare you suggest—"

"His death creates opportunity for you," she signed.

"His death breaks my heart," Viren said. If only Amaya could feel the ache in his chest to prove it.

Amaya glared back at him. "Then honor him. Find his children. That must be our top priority right now."

Viren's jaw clenched. How many times did he have to repeat this? "They're gone, Amaya. Captured by a Moonshadow elf—if they're not already dead, they will be soon. This is a time of crisis . . . An empty throne is a beacon of weakness. An invitation to destroy us. We must defend humanity against what's coming. I can help us from there." He pointed to the throne.

Amaya moved to block the throne and shook her head. That ache in Viren's chest throbbed.

"I know what you think, Amaya," Viren said, his voice rising. "You think I'm being an opportunist. But I couldn't be more selfless in my motivation. I am a servant of Katolis. I am a servant!"

"Those are awfully nice clothes for a humble servant, Viren," Amaya signed.

Viren stepped back. "You don't believe me? Then you take the throne. Go ahead, sit down. I'll support you as Queen Regent." He waved his hand at the empty seat.

But Amaya didn't bat an eye. "The throne stays empty until we find the boys," she signed.

Viren threw up his hands and stormed off.

Chapter 19
A Sweet Tooth and
An Iron Fist

Amaya made a point to visit the Valley of Graves every time she came to the capital of Katolis. She and Gren dismounted their horses in front of a monument not far from where Harrow's casket had burned the day before. The stone warrior was wearing full armor and riding a battle horse. Her gentle face had been lovingly sculpted, eyes closed peacefully and cropped hair spilling over her crown. One arm was extended downward as if to help up a fallen soldier.

"Hello, sister," Amaya signed. Gren gave her some space and she lit a ritual candle, then knelt before Sarai's statue and continued signing. "Sarai. Since before I can remember, you were my hero. The way I looked up to you, even then . . . you might as well have been carved out of marble. Perfect, strong, unwavering. Kind and true." She wiped a tear from her cheek. "I'm sorry, big sister. I failed you. I had your boys safe in my arms, but I let them slip through. But I swear to you, I will make this right. They will be found."

She bowed again, but her prayer was interrupted by shaking ground; a horse was approaching.

Amaya sighed. Could the high mage not even leave her alone with her dead sister?

"May I light a candle?" Viren asked Amaya.

His softness startled the general; it was such a change from his attitude in the throne room. Then again, Viren had known Sarai well too—perhaps better than Amaya even, in some ways. Amaya nodded, and Viren lit a candle.

"Your sister made him better," Viren said. "King Harrow told me he was never as strong or brave as Sarai believed him to be, but he tried every day to be stronger and braver so he could live up to what she saw in him."

Amaya nodded. It was hard to remain angry at anyone who complimented Sarai, even if it was Viren. "She was so compassionate and patient," she signed. "Unless of course you took the last jelly tart."

"I only made that mistake once," Viren said with a chuckle.

"A sweet tooth and an iron fist," Amaya signed. And they laughed a little more, like old times.

"General Amaya," Viren said. "I am sorry for what happened in the throne room. You helped me see the truth."

Amaya placed her hands on her hips. "And why was that so hard?"

"I was blinded by my abiding love of our kingdom, and of humanity itself," Viren continued, placing his hand on his heart.

Aaaaand, he's back, Amaya thought. She signed quickly.

"Guard! Fetch a stable boy, quickly," Gren translated. "I've encountered a substantial pile of bull—" Gren paused.

Amaya looked at him expectantly. "Say it," she signed.

"Bull . . . droppings," Gren finally translated.

Viren smirked, acknowledging Amaya's joke at his expense. "Yes, yes, go ahead and make fun of me," Viren said. "But believe me, I know the princes come first. Finding them is absolutely the top priority of the kingdom of Katolis."

"Good," she signed. "You see it my way. I'll be departing at sundown with a rescue party to find the princes."

"Of course," Viren said. "But allow me to ask—what happens to the Breach? You said yourself how precarious the situation is. Without you there commanding the fortress, do you believe in your heart that the border will hold?"

"Make your point, Viren," Amaya signed.

"My point is that if the Breach falls, the enemy will surge into Katolis," Viren said. "And I can hardly imagine the death and destruction that will ensue."

Unfortunately, Amaya knew that Viren was correct. Holding the Breach was a matter of life and death for thousands. "What are you suggesting we do?" Amaya signed.

"You return to the border, hold it fast. It's where you're needed most," Viren said. "A party of our best will be dispatched immediately to find the princes."

Amaya grimaced but said nothing. She didn't wholly trust Viren to rescue the princes, but she couldn't argue with his point. She was needed at the border.

"And in case you still doubt my intentions," Viren said, "I will task my own children, Soren and Claudia, with leading the rescue expedition."

"I do doubt your intentions," Amaya signed. *I just don't know what to do about it.* She approached Viren, stepping into the shadow of Sarai's statue. *What would you have done, sister?*

Amaya listened with her heart, then spoke up.

"I will return to the Breach. But your children won't lead the rescue, Viren—the mission will be assigned to Commander Gren." This plan felt like a rational compromise to Amaya. As general, she had a responsibility to the border and the people that she could not forsake for personal reasons ... but if she left Gren in charge, well, he had never let her down before.

Gren translated the words out loud before the meaning sank in. "Wait ... Commander Gren. That's me," he said. He raised his eyebrows and smiled with a mixture of surprise and pleasure at the new responsibility.

Viren glared at Gren, then Amaya. "All right."

CHAPTER 20
THE RAPIDS

Rayla clung to the deck. She was sure her face was as green as moonberry leaves right now. How could the princes actually enjoy rowing and floating along like this? And Bait seemed to especially be enjoying the ride. He hung off the back of the boat, playfully batting at water bugs and dipping his snout into the water.

"Bait! You know you're not supposed to do that," Ezran said. "No playing in the water." He pulled Bait back into the boat and shook his finger at him like a disappointed parent.

Callum leaned over to Rayla and whispered, "Bait loves the water, but he should be afraid of it."

Rayla glared at Callum. This was no time for a zoology lesson. The boat lurched and she cupped a hand over her mouth.

"Do you want to know why he's named Bait?" Callum asked.

"No, not particularly," Rayla managed to say through her fingers.

"Well, I'll tell you anyway," Callum said. "Glow toads? They're apparently . . . delicious."

"Gross," Rayla muttered.

"Deep-sea fishermen use them to catch giant fish, stuff like that. That's why he's named Bait. Get it? That's my stepdad's sense of humor." Callum laughed. "But that's why we have to be extra careful about him not getting in the water."

"Okay," Rayla said. "No glow toads in the water. Got it." The boat lurched again, and she cupped both hands over her mouth.

"Hey, you doing all right?" Callum asked.

Rayla didn't answer—she was afraid of what might happen if she took her hands from her mouth.

"Tell you what," Callum said. "I'm going to ask you five questions. That way, you won't have to think about your gut-wrenching seasickness."

Rayla braved moving her hands. "Please don't do that," she said.

"Come on, it'll be a fun distraction," Callum said.

Fine, Rayla thought. She was too sick to argue. "Five questions—that's all you get."

Callum beamed. What should he start with?

"Okay. Question one," he said. "We always heard all these crazy things about Xadia. Like it was this place with magic everywhere. Is that really what it's like?"

"Yes," Rayla said. "Next question." But when she faced the boys, Callum saw a little light in her eyes.

"It just must be so weird that everywhere you look ... there's magic," Callum said. His knowledge of magic was limited to things he'd seen Claudia do—mostly dark magic. It was hard to imagine any other kind.

"It's not weird," Rayla said, perking up. "In Xadia, magic is pretty much in everything. It's no different from saying, 'Everywhere you look, there's nature.' It's just ... part of the vibrancy or spirit of things, you know?"

Callum felt a new burst of energy and pulled on the oars extra hard. "I can't wait to see that. It sounds incredible."

"Yeah. Yeah, it is," Rayla said, smiling for the first time since boarding the boat.

"See, it's working, right?" Callum said. "Don't you feel a little better?"

Rayla raised her eyebrows. "Maybe so. Ask your next question."

"Okay, question two. What are your parents like?" But as soon as he'd asked the question, he could tell he'd made a huge mistake. Rayla turned away, the smile wiped off her face, and laid down in the boat.

"My parents are gone," she said. "They're dead."

"Oh. Rayla, I didn't mean to—"

"It's fine."

An awkward silence filled the air, and Callum looked out over the river, trying to get past the uncomfortable moment.

That's interesting, he thought. They were moving a lot faster than he'd realized.

"Hmmm," he said out loud.

"What is it now?" Rayla asked.

Callum considered how best to break the news. "So, this might not be the best time to bring this up. But are you sure you're not scared of the water?"

"I'm done with questions," Rayla said.

"Yeah, I know, I just…the water's about to get— Look!" Callum yelled.

Rayla turned to where Callum was pointing downriver. The water was much rougher down there, speeding along with rocks, twists, and whitewater. She bolted upright.

"Pull the boat over!" Rayla commanded. She crawled as far back in the boat as she could go.

"I don't think there's time," Callum said.

"Pull it over—I admit it! I hate the water, I'm afraid of it, it makes me sick. All the bad feelings," Rayla said, as if Callum could stop the inevitable if she only confessed to her phobia.

"It's too late, I'm sorry," Callum said. "Hang on!"

Rayla gripped the boat as it took a sudden dip over a short waterfall, heading into roaring rapids. She opened her mouth to scream but no sound came out. Next to her, Ezran and Callum shrieked with delight as the water splashed over them, though Ezran held tight to his knapsack with the egg in it.

"Keep holding," Callum yelled.

Rayla gritted her teeth as the boat careened through the

whitewater. They hopped over stones and thumped over logs, rushing with the turns of the river. She closed her eyes and tried to find her inner calm like Runaan had taught her, but her hand was throbbing from gripping the boat.

Finally, the boat tumbled down one last waterfall and then, as suddenly as they had started, the rapids ended.

Callum and Ezran pulled themselves into upright positions. Callum's heart was beating hard, but he was energized. He hadn't braved rapids like that since his father-sons bonding trip with King Harrow and Ezran years ago. He'd been scared then . . . like Rayla was today. She was lying on her back in the boat, drenched and clearly exhausted.

"You faced your fear!" Callum said. "Now that you've been through the worst of it, do you feel better about water?"

"I have never felt worse about water," Rayla said. "How would being through the worst make me feel better?"

"Well, anyway . . . We're making great time," Callum said. He thought it was best in moments like these to focus on the bright side.

"Hey, guys? Does anyone see Bait?" Ezran asked.

The three looked in every corner of the little boat for Bait, but he was nowhere to be found. Callum scanned the water and finally spotted the little yellow blob.

"Over there!" he shouted. Bait had evidently been bumped from the boat during their wild ride and was just now catching up, bouncing down the last of the rapids. They watched as he fell headlong down the waterfall, landing some distance from the boat. He bobbed up and down like a buoy.

"Bait! Come back here, you need to be inside this boat," Ezran yelled. "Do your widdle froggy-paddle." Ezran mimed swimming to Bait, who copied him.

Callum slowed the boat to a crawl with an oar, and Bait flapped his toad legs as fast as he could, slowly closing the space between himself and the boat.

Rayla shook her head. This was unbelievable. "I see how it is now. Stop the boat for the grumpy toad, but not for the cheery, positive-attitude elf."

Still, she had to admit she was relieved when Bait reached the boat and Ezran scooped him up.

"You know you're not supposed to get in the water," Ezran said as he rubbed noses with Bait.

"What a disaster," Rayla said. She collapsed back onto the boat floor, where she noticed something strange—the rune cube was glowing.

"Hey, guys," Rayla said and pointed at the cube.

Callum followed her finger. Sure enough, one of the runes was pulsing with light.

"Hey, that's the Ocean rune," Callum said. He picked up the cube and the light dimmed. *Odd.* He moved the cube closer to the bottom of the boat and the rune glowed again. Was there some kind of primal magic in the river?

BAM! Something hit the boat from below and sent it shooting up into the air. Before he knew it, Callum was looking straight into the jaws of a giant green river monster. It snapped its teeth but just missed the boat and its occupants.

Callum, Ezran, and Bait landed downstream with a tremendous splash. Where was Rayla?

Over on shore, Rayla didn't care that a huge monster had just attacked them—she was glad to have been flipped back onto dry land. "Sweet solid land, we meet again. How I've missed your solidness," Rayla said. She kissed the ground with glee.

A huge splash turned her attention back to the river. Callum and Ezran were swimming for land and it looked like they would make it. But the huge river monster had no interest in the human princes—it had set its hungry eyes on a tasty, glowing yellow-and-blue morsel—Bait.

Rayla cupped her hands over her mouth and yelled, "Hey, guys, behind you, Bait is in trouble."

The monster dove down after Bait, who moved out of the way at the last second.

But Callum and Ezran seemed oblivious to the danger.

Rayla waved her arms at the boys. She'd have to yell louder over the splashing. "Bait is in trouble!" she shouted. Ezran finally heard her.

"What?!" he shouted.

"Bait needs help!" Rayla repeated.

"Bait sneezed kelp?" Ezran asked.

"No," Callum shouted to Ezran. "She says, 'Bait's knees smell.'"

"Well, that's just mean," Ezran said.

"No!" Rayla cried out. Seriously—it was one frustration after another with these boys.

The river monster lunged at Bait again. This time Bait

leaped and landed on the side of the monster's face.

This was not going well.

"It's down to me, isn't it? Of course it is," Rayla said to herself. She buried her face in her hands. "Goodbye, sweet solid land. I barely knew you..."

And with that, Rayla leaped into the river and landed on a slippery, floating log. She took a moment to get her bearings and then stood up with her blades drawn.

"Come on, Rayla, do it for the frog," she said. "The grumpy frog that hates you. Here goes!"

Just then, the river monster threw its green, scaly head back, tossing Bait high into the air. As Bait plummeted back toward the water, the monster opened its jaws to catch him in its mouth. Rayla flipped from the log and into its mouth, jamming its jaws open with her blades. Bait landed on Rayla's head instead of in the creature's gullet.

But Rayla didn't have time to celebrate that victory. The monster nosedived deep below the surface, trying to shake Rayla from its jaws. Rayla squeezed Bait in her arms and tried not to think about seasickness, river monsters, or drowning. She'd never been underwater for so long. Her lungs felt like they might burst.

Do something, Rayla.

With a burst of courage, she managed to scramble out of the creature's jaws and hook one blade into the folds of its leathery skin just as they broke the surface again. The creature thrashed about and Rayla hung on tight, with Bait hanging on to her. She glanced at the shore. Where were those boys? She could use a little help.

Meanwhile, Ezran and Callum managed to pull themselves out of the water, where they could finally see that Bait and Rayla were in major trouble. Thinking quickly, Callum lifted the primal stone with one hand and traced a glowing rune shape in the air with the other. Powerful electricity began sparking around his hand, just as it had before.

Ezran saw his brother's stance. *Uh-oh.*

"Why would you even attempt to do that again after this morning?" he asked.

"I have an idea," Callum said. "And it doesn't require knowing any Draconic."

Before Ezran could stop him, Callum yelled across the water. "Rayla, jump!"

"But you don't know how to—" Rayla shouted back.

"Never mind, just jump!" Callum repeated.

Rayla decided she didn't have anything to lose. She propelled herself and Bait into the air just as Callum plunged his electrified hand into the water.

Zap!! The electricity traveled through the water and hit the monster with a mighty shock. It fell back into the water and made a quick getaway.

A moment later, Rayla and Bait plummeted back into the river. They swam to shore where Callum and Ezran were.

"Rayla, you saved Bait," Ezran said, reaching out for the toad with his face full of gratitude. Then he covered Bait's ears. "Without you, he would have been fish food."

"That was really brave, Rayla," Callum said.

Rayla stood up and shook her head. "No, I already told you. I'm afraid of water."

"I know. That's why doing what you did was so heroic," Callum explained.

"Oh." *Really?* "Thanks," she said. She sat down on a nearby rock and started wringing out water from her hair.

"Why wouldn't you just tell us about your fear before?" Ezran asked. He took a seat near her and Callum came over too. "It's okay to be afraid of things."

Rayla thought for a moment. Why had she held back? "I guess . . . I was afraid of being afraid," she finally said. It sounded funny, but it was the truth.

"That's kind of circular," Callum said with a philosophical air. "But worth noting: You're not afraid of being afraid of being afraid." He squinted and nodded slowly as he said this so it would sound more like timeless wisdom.

Rayla rolled her eyes. "That's deep, Callum," she said. "But stupid."

Callum laughed.

"The thing is," Rayla continued, shifting her position on the rock. "Moonshadow elves aren't supposed to show fear. Ever."

"That's sad," Ezran said.

Rayla closed her eyes and took a deep breath. *Maybe it is sad. But . . .* "It's just our way," she said.

Ezran leaned in. "I know elves have different ways, but I'll tell you something my dad always says."

On hearing the king mentioned, Rayla instinctively

fidgeted with the ribbon-binding on her wrist.

Ezran continued, doing his best to impersonate the king's deep voice. "He says, 'Feelings are feelings, and there's never shame or weakness in your heart's truth.'"

Rayla thought those words were beautiful. *Beautiful, and so different from what I was always taught.*

She decided it was time to tell the truth, if not about their father, then about her own father and mother. "I've got something to tell you both. My parents aren't actually dead, but I wish they were. Because they're cowards."

The boys looked at her, shocked. "What do you mean?" Callum asked.

Rayla felt a heaviness in her belly; talking about her parents always hurt. "My parents were part of an elite force, the Dragonguard—elven warriors chosen to protect the egg of the Dragon Prince. You might not know this, but storm dragons only lay an egg once every thousand years, give or take a century. So that egg is so rare and precious." She pointed to the egg in Ezran's knapsack. "Being part of the guard was a great honor. But when the humans came and killed the Dragon King, the Dragonguard failed in their duty." She hung her head. "They weren't killed. My parents ran away. I'm so ashamed of them."

But Callum shook his head. "Rayla, I'm sorry for what humans did."

She ignored his apology. "So, you see, that's why I have to make things right. When I first left Xadia, I was on a quest for revenge. But the moment I saw that egg, everything changed. Now? This is a journey of redemption."

"We're in this journey together," Callum said. He put a hand on her shoulder.

Rayla appreciated the gesture, but she was reaching her limit on this mushy stuff. She turned toward the water . . . and saw their boat floating away.

"Oh no," she said, feigning worry. She ran to the shore and pretended to try to grab the boat. "Ooops. It slipped just out of my reach. What will we do now?" Not so secretly, Rayla was thrilled the boat might get lost forever.

But the boat reversed and drifted back toward her. Callum and Ezran laughed. Then Callum walked over and kicked the boat away with his foot.

"Goodbye, boat."

Rayla let out a sigh of relief and unconscioulsly fidgeted with her binding again. "Thank you," she said.

"So, what is the deal with your wrist ribbon thing? Does it mean something?" Callum asked.

"Uh . . ." For a moment Rayla considered letting it all out. She could tell these boys, she thought. She trusted them enough. But when she finally spoke, all she said was "Nah. It doesn't mean anything. Just decorative." She covered the ribbon with her unbound hand.

Callum sensed a sudden change in her tone from just a few minutes before. "Decorative?" he asked.

"Yeah. Moonshadow elf thing, I guess," Rayla said, looking away.

Callum nodded, but he wasn't convinced. "Hmm. Okay."

CHAPTER 21
WISHES AND COMMANDS

It was late in the day and most of the castle denizens had begun to settle in for the evening, but a garrison of Katolis soldiers gathered near the great castle gates. Amaya was preparing to return to the Breach with her troops, but first she needed to brief the rescue party.

"I've sent word to Corvus that the king has passed," she signed to Gren and another officer. "Corvus will be expecting you and the rescue party within a day or two."

"Very good. And is Lord Viren aware that Corvus has been tracking the princes?" the officer asked.

"No," Amaya signed. Corvus was her insurance against Viren's treacherous ways. She leaned in close to Gren. "Do not trust Viren," she signed. "It may be a month from now, it may be a year from now—but he *will* stab you in the back."

"I'll be careful," Gren said.

Amaya put a finger up to his lips to drive home her point. Then she signed warmly to Gren: "I trust you. You have been my voice. Now I need you to be my will and save those boys." She wrapped her arms around him in a hug.

"You find those boys, Gren—bring them home," Amaya signed as she mounted her horse.

"Yes, General. Your wish is my command," Gren said.

Amaya signed back for added clarity. "It is a command."

Gren smiled. He would miss his general's wisdom, but also her humor.

Just then, Viren and Soren appeared. All traces of warmth vanished from Amaya's face.

"I expect to be notified when the princes are found and safe," she signed to Viren.

Viren bowed in assent. "I'll send word to the Breach immediately."

Amaya gave Viren one last intimidating look and then galloped off, her troops behind her. Gren could still see them in the distance when Soren sidled up to him.

"Bad news, Gren," Soren said, an exaggerated frown on his face. "Change of plans."

"What are you talking about?" Gren asked.

Soren smirked but said nothing further, so Gren turned to Viren.

"What's he talking about, Viren?"

"Oh, I've decided you're off the mission," Viren said. "Soren will lead the expedition."

"What?" Gren said. "General Amaya was very specific that I was to lead this." Gren was sure of that.

"Nothing to worry about, Commander," Viren said. "Perhaps there was a misunderstanding. But you and I do need to have a talk."

"Oh, of course," Gren said. If there was a misunderstanding, they needed to get to the bottom of it right away. "Communication is the key to high-performance teamwork."

"Soren, set up a meeting for Commander Gren and me to discuss his concerns—somewhere quiet. Say, around nine tonight," Viren said.

"Yes, very good," Gren said. "Nine suits my schedule."

"Very good," Viren said. "See you then."

Viren walked slowly down the spiral stairs to the dungeon. He gripped the railing hard and leaned on his staff. It had been a long day. At the bottom of the stairs he saw Gren, who had been chained to the wall, just as Viren had ordered.

"Five past nine," Viren said. "I apologize for my tardiness."

"It was only five minutes," Gren said.

"So, what are your concerns?" Viren asked.

"Well—" Gren coughed. "You took me off the mission."

"Noted," Viren said. "Go on."

"And you threw me in this dungeon," Gren said.

"Ah, I see," Viren said. "Anything else?"

Gren thought for a moment. "Nope," he said. "I guess those are the main two concerns."

"Thank you," Viren said. "Your feedback is a gift." He bowed deeply and smiled to himself. This freckle-faced goof was going to be the easiest prisoner he'd ever encountered.

As Viren straightened up, Claudia came running down the dungeon hall.

"Father," she said. "It's about our other prisoner." She beckoned for Viren to follow her.

Claudia pushed opened a door to a smaller dungeon cell, where the leader of the elven assassins sat on the ground, his head bowed, his wrists in chains.

"He's still refusing to eat," Claudia said to her father.

Viren sighed and turned away. And this elf was probably going to be the hardest. "Then let him be hungry."

chapter 22
the tracker

Rayla lay curled on a tree branch above the boys. All night she'd been tossing and turning—the ribbon on her wrist was definitely starting to constrict blood flow to her hand. It was turning purple and her fingers had become unnaturally clawed.

She closed her eyes for what seemed like the thousandth time and tried to relax.

Snap.

It was the tiniest sound, not enough to wake the sleeping boys or even the squirrel resting near her, but the little crunch put Rayla on high alert. That crack was a twig snapping, Rayla was almost sure of it—and it had been snapped by a human foot, one that was trying to tread silently.

Rayla sprang to her feet, grabbed her blades, and sprinted into the forest.

It took her only a few minutes to find the broken twig. She knelt down and picked it up, then heard rustling in a nearby bush. She crouched and whipped out her blades. There was another rustle and Rayla's shoulders tensed . . . until a dainty fawn appeared and wagged its ears.

Rayla breathed a sigh of relief and put away her blades. She reached her hand toward the fawn.

"Aw . . . you scared me, wee cutie," she said.

The baby deer stared back at Rayla, then cautiously approached and sniffed her fingers. Rayla stroked one of its brown ears and the deer nuzzled her injured hand in return, licking the purplish skin.

"Thanks, little one, but my hand has a problem you can't lick away," Rayla said.

Suddenly, the deer backed away from Rayla. It stared above Rayla's head and flattened its ears.

"What's the matter?" Rayla asked. But the deer jumped into the bushes. Rayla looked over her shoulder just in time to see a trapping net descend from the tree above. She scrambled on the ground as a tall, dark figure dropped down from the trees, holding a weapon that looked like a bladed fleur-de-lis attached to a long chain. He twirled it above his head, getting ready to throw.

"Never trapped an elf before," he said. "It's going to be easier than I thought."

Rayla had dodged the net just enough that only her legs and

torso were entwined. She used her arms to maneuver her body away from the blow of the grappling hook, and it sank into the ground next to her. She quickly looped the net around the hook. When her attacker pulled the chain up, he inadvertently yanked the net off Rayla.

Standing now, Rayla snapped her blades open, ready to confront the human threat. She took a deep breath and ran straight at her attacker.

The human deflected Rayla's blades with his hook, putting her on the defensive. She backflipped away from him and then hopped onto a high tree branch. Up in the trees, Rayla could take this human out of his comfort zone and attack a sure weak spot—his balance.

Corvus appreciated the elf's ingenuity, but the trick was on her; a little tree climbing didn't scare him. He used his grappling hook and chain as assists and began the ascent. Once on the same level as the elf, he whipped his weapon around and snagged her around her foot. She dangled upside down from the branch, held by his chain.

"Give me the boys peacefully and I'll let you go," Corvus said, yanking the chain to pull the elf up even higher in the air. "Release your prisoners."

Rayla didn't appreciate his tone. "They're not my prisoners," she said. "They choose to travel with me."

"What? Why would they trust *you*?" the human asked. Then without warning, he released his hold on Rayla's foot and she tumbled down to the branch below.

"Because we're in this together. They're my friends now," she said, feeling much more defensive about this than she expected.

"Friends. Am I missing something?" the human asked. "You killed their father."

"I didn't kill anyone," Rayla said. It surprised her that she was so proud of this fact.

"Your leader did. What's the difference?" the human asked, twirling his weapon. He hurled the blade and broke the branch that Rayla was standing on. She screamed as she dropped down, but managed to catch another branch with her arms.

She was still holding both blades, but her injured hand was stiffening with each second. With a cry of frustration, Rayla dropped one blade and watched it tumble to the forest floor.

Corvus saw his chance. Whether this elf had killed King Harrow or not, it was ridiculous to think the princes would befriend any elf, let alone one from the team that killed their father. He swung over to the elf and pressed his tracker's boot onto her arm.

"Wait, they don't even know about their father, do they?" Corvus realized aloud.

Rayla didn't respond. She summoned her remaining strength to swing herself up onto the branch one-handed and sent the human tumbling down the branches. She leaped over to the top of a cliff.

"When they find out, they'll hate you," the human said, following her onto the rocky overlook.

"Shut up," Rayla cried. This tracker was getting under her skin.

He hurled his weapon again and it wrapped around Rayla's blade. But instead of trying to free her blade, Rayla used both her hands to pull the human toward her. She looked down over the cliff's edge and made a split-second decision. She flipped off the mountainside, taking the human with her. The two keeled over the ravine, bouncing off rocks and tree branches on the way down.

The human twisted and turned to lessen the blow of his fall, but he ended up at the bottom of the gorge, covered in wet, sticky mud. Rayla, on the other hand, stopped her fall by sticking her single blade into some rock on higher ground. She looked down at the human with her hands on her hips.

"Savor your victory, elf. Next time you won't be so lucky," the tracker warned.

Rayla saw her chance to deliver one last blow. "Says the guy in the ditch!" she jeered. Then she sprinted back toward camp.

As she ran, fear coursed through her veins. But was she afraid of the human attacking her again, or that he would show up and tell the princes the truth? Because Rayla couldn't help but wonder—would everything change when Callum and Ezran found out their father was dead?

Ezran rubbed the crusted sleep from his eyes and stretched his arms over his head. Then he surveyed the camp. Callum and Bait were sleeping soundly but Rayla was nowhere to be found.

"Callum, wake up," Ezran said, shaking his brother's shoulder. "I think we're alone."

"Alone at last," Callum responded, but he wasn't really awake. He appeared to be lost in a dream, snuggled up to a loaf of bread they'd stolen from the Banther Lodge. They had put Callum in charge of the bread, but Ezran thought he was taking his job a little too seriously—he had his arms around it in an embrace and his lips were pressed up against it. Ezran shook Callum again.

"What?! What is it?" Callum asked. He sat straight up.

"Wake up! Rayla's missing," Ezran said.

"Oh no—did she take it?" Callum asked. He looked around feverishly for the dragon egg.

"No, don't worry. It's still right here," Ezran said. He lifted his blanket a little to reveal the egg, safe and sound and softly glowing underneath.

"Okay good," Callum breathed, relaxing a little bit. "But that still doesn't mean we can trust her. I mean, it's weird that she just leaves camp without telling either of us. What do you think she's doing?"

"I like her, Callum," Ezran said. "I think maybe we should trust her. She wants the same things we want."

"I like her too," Callum said. "But the thing is, she's—"

"An elf? Who cares?" Ezran said. "It seems like maybe everything we ever heard about elves is wrong."

"No. Don't get so defensive," Callum said. "I was going to say, the thing is, she's not telling us everything. I can feel it. We have to be careful, okay?"

Ezran looked at Rayla's empty branch. It *was* sort of weird she kept leaving camp alone. He turned back to Callum and nodded.

Suddenly, Rayla rushed back into camp. "Go, go, go! We've gotta move," she barked.

"What's going on? Where were you?" Callum asked.

And now the elf was bossing them around. Ezran hadn't even had breakfast. "We should really eat something before we leave," Ezran said. "Look how grumpy Bait is right now." He picked up Bait to show Rayla and Callum his sour face, which honestly was no grumpier than usual, which is to say it was awfully sour.

"There's no time to eat," Rayla said. "We have to get moving now."

"Rayla, why?" Callum asked. "You have to at least explain—"

"I don't have to explain anything to you," Rayla snapped. She picked up Callum's empty backpack and shoved it into his chest. "Pack up! Let's go!"

"Fine," Callum said, and opened his pack.

Ezran followed his lead. He gently swaddled the egg and slid it in his own backpack. Then he heaved the bag onto his back. Had the egg been this heavy yesterday?

Callum stuffed the primal stone, sketchbook, and pencil into his bag. The pack seemed full, but still he felt like he was forgetting something.

"Come on, you two! Hurry," Rayla said.

"Okay, relax—we're coming," Callum said. Ezran scooped up Bait and they ran to catch up to Rayla.

CHAPTER 23
SECRET MISSIONS

Soren bounded up the tower's stone steps, taking them two at a time. He had been a sickly child, but that was years ago. These days, he was never one to waste an opportunity for exercise; he had been in a full sprint ever since a guard informed him his father would like a meeting.

He emerged on the highest level of the castle's battlements. His father stood there waiting, hands clasped behind his back, surveying the vast mountains and valleys of Katolis.

"Whew! Hey, Dad," Soren said, catching his breath. "I love having meetings up here. I get a killer leg workout going up all those stairs." He decided to continue his workout and began doing lunges.

"We have important things to discuss," his father said. "Try and focus." He turned around to face Soren.

"No problem, Dad," Soren said. "You have my undivided attention." He bent down to touch his toes.

Viren had always wished for a son—someone he could mold in his own likeness, a mind much like his own, to whom he could pass all his wisdom. He sighed. Soren was not such a son. "This evening you and your sister depart on a mission," he said.

"Yep, I know," Soren said. "Searching for the princes." He touched his toes again, head between his legs. "Oh yeah, that's the good kind of burn."

Viren spoke to the back of his son's head. "The outcome of your mission is critical to the future of our kingdom." He planted his staff on the stones for emphasis. "Do you understand?"

"We got this, Dad. We'll find them," Soren promised.

"I'm sure you will find them. And your confidence is inspiring," Viren continued. "But there's a bit of... nuance to this situation."

"No idea what *nuance* is," Soren said, tilting into a quad stretch.

Well, then Viren would have to be as direct as he could. "Listen closely," he said, leaning in toward Soren's ear. "You are to return with the terrible news that the princes have perished."

Soren stopped mid-stretch and stood up. He couldn't have heard that right. "Excuse me? I think my head was upside down and it got sort of mixed up. Can you say that again?"

His father looked directly into his eyes and repeated, "You are to return with the terrible news that both princes have died."

"So, hold up," Soren said, still trying to wrap his mind around his father's insinuations. "If we return with news that they're dead, won't it mean we failed our mission?"

Viren shook his head. This was going to be even harder than he thought. He would have to remain delicate in his phrasing; if he could make Soren understand the gravity of their situation and the bigger picture, perhaps it would take the sting out of what he was asking him to do. "The coming war will determine the fate of humanity. History has come to a crucial tipping point..." he began. He paused, scrutinizing Soren's face to see if he understood.

"So, you're saying, things could go either way," Soren said.

"Yes, precisely," Viren said, momentarily impressed.

"Like a seesaw!" Soren shouted out.

Viren blinked twice, amazed at the folly of his own offspring. "Yes. If that helps you. History is like ... a seesaw," he said. "If we are strong enough to make the right decisions, humans may finally return to Xadia and take back the great magical lands that are rightfully ours. But if we are led by a child king—"

"He'll make bad choices?" Soren asked.

"He will make weak choices," Viren corrected. "If we make mistakes and history tips the wrong way—the forces of Xadia will crush not only Katolis, but all the five kingdoms."

"I get it," Soren said. "Well, most of it. So, I'm supposed to come back with the news that they're dead." He scratched his chin. "What I don't understand is what am I supposed to do if we find them alive?" Soren was afraid he knew the answer already, but he wanted to hear his father say it.

His father looked him in the eye. "Oh, son, you'll know the right thing to do." A dark shadow fell over his face.

So . . . that *was* what his father meant.

Soren shook his head. "I don't know. I don't know if I can do that." Ridiculing the princes was a part of his daily life, but he adored Callum and Ezran. He hoped they were still alive.

"Out there, in the wild, accidents happen every day," his father continued. "Deadly accidents." He placed one hand on Soren's cheek and tilted his face upward. "My son. This won't be easy, but you are strong."

Soren's insides knotted up, but he nodded.

Viren tapped his staff on the ground one more time. "Tell no one, Soren. Not even Claudia. You must carry this weight alone." *Of course*, Viren thought, *there isn't anything to tell.* Only insinuation. He was a careful man.

Viren looked away from Soren and turned back to gaze at the vista. "There is no joy in this. It will be a burden for me to take the throne. And someday that throne will belong to you."

Meanwhile, Claudia waited in her father's study. She had removed the drape from the mysterious runic mirror and was feverishly attempting to unearth its secrets. Her father would be so proud if she could figure it out alone.

She traced the ancient runes along the mirror's front with her long, painted fingernails. Then she jiggled open one of her father's desk drawers and extracted a bowl. From a nearby shelf she pulled down a crystal container and a pair of tweezers. Carefully, she removed a single dried lizard's tongue and placed it in the bowl. Then she sprinkled blue dust on the tongue and began to chant. Claudia loved this spell because it caused inanimate objects to literally speak. In the past, she had wasted a few of these tiny tongues on her own amusement; it was satisfying to use one on something that really mattered.

"Speak your true nature to me," Claudia commanded. Then she uttered the strange words to initiate the spell: "Cigam ruoy laever."

The blue dust began to glow, and Claudia's eyes turned purple. A flash of purple light seized the room momentarily. Then, nothing.

"You are a stubborn magic mirror," she said.

"You think I haven't tried that?" her father asked.

Claudia whirled around. How long had her father been standing there?

"I've cast eight different 'reveal' spells, and they all failed," her father said. He walked up to the mirror and stood next to Claudia. "At the end, I see nothing but my own frustrated face staring back at me."

Claudia spoke to her father in the mirror's reflection. "Maybe . . . it's just a mirror," she said.

"Of all the treasures, artifacts, and relics in the lair of the Dragon King and Queen, they kept this closest to where they slept," her father said. He ran his hand over the golden frame. "It must be important."

"Then we'll figure it out," Claudia said. "Whatever it takes. Hear that, mirror? I'm putting you on notice." She held two fingers to her eyes and then pointed them back at the mirror.

Viren shook his head. At least this child was bright, but her endless quirks were insufferable. He covered the mirror with the drape.

"We have something important to discuss," he said. "Your mission."

"To rescue the princes," Claudia said.

"Yes, but you will have a secret mission that is far more important." Her father leaned in close. "Claudia, you must recover that dragon egg."

"Well, Dad, the princes have it with them, so it shouldn't be a problem," Claudia said. She loved her dad but sometimes he needed to lighten up a little. "Princes, egg . . . I've got room for a third mission, if you need anything while we're out," she said with a wry smile.

Her father ignored her. "The egg cannot fall into the wrong hands," he said. "It is too powerful, too dangerous. Whatever happens, whatever accidents or . . . tragedies may occur, above all else you must return with that egg."

"I understand," Claudia said.

"Good."

"One question," Claudia added. "Let's say, in the unlikely event we're attacked by giant bumble-scorps, and they're all buzzing and flailing their scorps at us..." Claudia made a buzzing noise with her lips and began circling her father.

"Claudia, bumble-scorps only attack when people are alone," her father interrupted. "Stick with your brother and you'll be fine."

"Yeah, I know, but say there's some sort of crazy, brazen bumble-scorp that attacks both of us, and I'm forced to choose between saving the egg . . . and saving Soren. What should I do?"

Her father stared at her, stone-faced.

"Dad—it's a joke. Relax, I'm kidding." Claudia made another loud buzzing sound to show him she was only teasing. "Everything will be fine." She turned to walk out of the study.

"The egg," her father said.

Claudia paused but didn't turn around. *What?*

"If you must choose . . . choose the egg."

CHAPTER 24
THE MEGABURP
OF DOOM

After an hour or so of walking, the princes, elf, and glow toad emerged from the forest into a valley. Steep, snowy mountains loomed on either side of them, but straight ahead there was a smooth, trodden trail. Callum observed the well-worn walkway, relieved that someone else had followed this path.

"Wait. This path is too easy," Rayla said. She put up a hand to stop them from walking farther.

"No, it's not. It's exactly the right amount of easy," Callum said.

"Listen to me," Rayla said. "The trail is well-worn, it's flat, it's soft. Sooner or later we're going to run into somebody." She turned and pointed straight up the mountainside. "We need to go that way. Tougher terrain is safer for us. The tougher the better."

"That sounds terrible," Callum said.

"Exactly!" Rayla replied. "Terrible is perfect."

Ezran happened to agree with Callum. "This is already tough enough," he said, trying to keep the whine out of his voice. "Do you have any idea how heavy this egg is?" He tugged on his pack's shoulder straps, which he feared were making permanent indentations in his skin.

Rayla gave Ezran a look. "Uh, no, I don't have any idea—*because you won't trust me to carry it.*"

Ezran looked at Callum. What was he supposed to say to that?

"Should we trust you?" Callum asked Rayla. She was touching that ribbon thing again. "Have you told us the truth about everything?" He looked her in the eye.

Rayla met Callum's gaze and held it for a long while, as if trying to decide what to say.

"Ugh, fine," she finally said, breaking the stare. "Keep carrying the extremely heavy egg. But quit crying about it; we're going this way." She turned and started up a rocky path.

Once again, Ezran and Callum followed.

Back at the castle, Claudia made her way to the courtyard, her father's words echoing in her mind. He couldn't have been serious about choosing the egg over her own brother, could he?

No, she decided. Her father was under a lot of stress; best to take everything he said right now with a grain of salt.

She emerged outside and was glad to find Soren sitting on a bench next to a platter of jelly tarts. He was staring into space, methodically popping tarts into his mouth.

"Hey, Sor-bear. What's wrong? You look kind of down," Claudia said. She ruffled his hair. "Grizzly Sor-bear."

"Did Dad say anything . . . strange to you?" Soren asked.

Claudia looked away, unsure of where the conversation was headed. "Yeah, he kind of did. Did he say anything to you?"

Soren paused and shoveled another jelly tart into his mouth. He wasn't sure how to broach the subject of being ordered to murder the princes. Finally, he decided it was best not to get into it. "No. Nope, totally not. Just the standard Dad chat. He didn't say anything weird to me."

Claudia furrowed her brow. "Oh. Okay, I guess."

"So, what did he say to you that was so strange?" Soren asked.

But now Claudia wasn't sure she wanted to share her information either. She noticed a nearby squirrel eating a walnut.

"Uh, he said that walnuts are his favorite . . . fruit! I mean that's crazy, right?" she said. "Walnuts aren't even a fruit!"

Soren furrowed his brow and popped another jelly tart in his mouth.

"I mean, what's his favorite vegetable, ice cream?" Claudia continued. Then she laughed at her own joke and accidentally let out a snort. Her brother joined in—he could never keep it together when Claudia snorted.

"Anyway. Are you ready for our mission?" Claudia asked.

"Yeah. I guess I am," Soren said. He picked up the leftover jelly tarts. Talking with his sister had calmed him down, and all this stress eating was bad for his figure.

"Great. I'm sure you won't die," Claudia said.

Huh? Soren turned to his sister.

"On this mission," Claudia quickly added. "I mean, eventually you will die. I assume. But who knows? Maybe you won't."

"Thanks, Claudia," Soren said with a smile. It was sweet his little sister thought he might be immortal.

As the group climbed higher into the mountains, the wind whipped harshly around them. The snowdrifts had deepened, and the ice had slickened the farther they got up the mountain. Callum, Ezran, and Bait struggled to keep up with Rayla's pace.

Finally, Rayla paused and looked back at all the ground they'd covered. "All right, let's stop and eat," she said. "I'm starving."

"Finally," Ezran said, collapsing onto the snowy ground.

Callum dug his hand into his backpack for the bread. When he didn't come up with anything, he stuck his face in the pack and rifled around more vigorously. *Oh no.*

"I don't have the food," he admitted. "How could this happen?" He slapped his palm against his forehead.

"What?" Rayla asked. "You had one job, carry our food. How could you leave it?"

"You rushed us," Callum said. "You were yelling at us and I just . . . You made me leave it."

"You're blaming me for your mistake?" Rayla asked. "Explain to me how that works, please."

"Maybe. At least partially," Callum said.

"Oh, that's right, because I remember yelling three things," Rayla said. She unfurled three fingers from her good hand and counted off on them. "One, 'Hurry, hurry'. Two, 'Let's go, go, go.' And three, 'Be sure to abandon all the supplies you need to survive in the wild.'"

"What are we going to do?" Ezran cried. "We're out of food."

Callum swallowed. He was suddenly *starving*.

Rayla shook her head. This was too good an opportunity to pass up. "Well, sorry you won't be able to feast on the terrible-tasting rocklike lumps you humans call 'food,'" she said, "but I suppose I'd be willing to share my moonberry juice with you. Unless, of course, you're worried it might be blood . . ." She paused, but the boys didn't seem in the mood for joking around. She dropped the sarcasm. "You know, it's packed with super nutrients, and I still have plenty."

She dug into her bag and pulled out the glass bottle . . . only to find that it was empty!

"All right, which one of you stole it?" she said, holding up the bottle. "I knew I shouldn't trust humans."

The princes looked at her blankly.

"Come on, out with it. Which one of you went through my stuff?" she demanded.

"I didn't touch your things," Callum said.

"Don't look at me," Ezran said with palms facing up.

Rayla pondered the innocent looks on the princes' faces. Either they were masterful liars or they hadn't taken her juice. "Well, I didn't drink it," she said. "If one of you didn't sneak it, then—"

HIC.

"What's that?" Rayla asked. The three turned to the source of the juiciest hiccup they'd ever heard. Bait was glowing a deep shade of purplish red and licking his lips. He hiccupped again.

"Wait," Rayla said. "Did that little frog monster—"

"Bait wouldn't do that," Ezran said. "You have no reason to think—"

HIC, Bait bellowed again.

"Don't accuse him," Ezran said. He was intent on defending his pet, but he was feeling less and less sure of Bait's innocence.

"Look at how he's glowing," Rayla said.

"Well, Bait glows different ways depending on how he's feeling," Ezran said. Rayla maybe didn't understand that yet. "Like, he has one color if he's lonely. Or he glows another way if he's hungry." He walked over to Bait and sat down in front of him.

"So, what does this particular shade signify?" Rayla asked.

"Hmm," Ezran said. He was wondering that himself. "Actually, I've never seen him glow that color before. Kind of a reddish purplish . . . berry color."

UUURRRPPP. Bait let out a belch right in Ezran's face.

"Yeah, he drank it," Ezran said as the smell of moonberry juice washed over him.

Rayla shook her head, put the bottle away, and continued walking.

Everyone moved on in silence.

Hours later, Ezran adjusted the backpack on his shoulders. The farther up the mountain they had traveled, the deeper and more treacherous the snow had become. Rayla and Callum didn't know how easy they had it, what with their long legs and no heavy dragon egg on their backs.

"Rayla, can you slow down?" he gasped. "It's getting a little tricky."

Rayla ignored him, but Callum turned around and offered a hand to Ezran.

"Rayla! Come on," Callum said. "You're the one who made us take this crazy route, at least let us keep up with you." He was practically pulling his little brother—and the egg—up the mountain now.

Ezran suddenly let go and plopped down in the snow. "I just need to put the egg down a second and catch my breath," he said. Bait stopped to keep Ezran company.

"Stopping is not keeping up," Rayla said. Finally, she spun around to look at the princes. "There is a solution, you know. You can just let me carry the egg."

Callum shook his head. "That's not happening."

"You realize that I could just take it, right?" Rayla said. She crossed her arms. "I could just take it from you, any time I wanted."

"Yeah, that's good, Rayla. Way to increase trust," Callum said.

"But I haven't taken it—that's the point," she said.

"Oh, well, congratulations," Callum said. "You haven't threatened us and forced us to give you the egg? You deserve a medal; you're a hero!" He shouted the last word at the top of his lungs.

Ezran listened to the word echo throughout the mountain, and then another sound caught his ears. Small fissures were forming in a wall of ice nearby. He waved a hand to alert Rayla and Callum, but they were absorbed in their argument.

"Well, I could take it," Rayla shouted. "I could go return that egg all on my own, and as a matter of fact, I would be a hero," she said. "It would be glorious—I'd go down in Xadian history."

"Guys, you need to keep it down," Ezran whispered. He tugged on Callum's sleeve and pointed at the cracking snowdrifts above them, but neither Callum nor Rayla paid him any attention.

"Yup, I could take the egg from you," Rayla barreled on. "I'd be the most celebrated elf. They'd call me . . . the Egg Bringer!"

"Then take it," Callum screamed. "What's stopping you?"

"The fact that I actually want to stop this war," Rayla spat back. "The egg must come from you. Human princes, returning the egg to the Dragon Queen. That's the gesture that matters. That's the gesture that could end the war and change the world."

"Guys, SHHHHH," Ezran said as loudly as he dared, finally

grabbing their attention. "You guys need to stop fighting. Look." He pointed to the huge sheets of cracking ice. "All your yelling is breaking up the ice. If we're not careful, we could start an avalanche. Got it?"

Callum and Rayla both stopped yelling.

"Got it," Callum whispered.

"Not a peep," Rayla mouthed to Ezran.

"Good," Ezran said. He gave them the thumbs-up sign, put a finger to his lips, picked up the egg, and resumed walking up the mountain. Rayla and Callum followed behind silently.

But Bait stood still as a statue in the snow, a strange, almost pained look on his face. His cheeks puffed out, and his eyes bulged—he felt something coming. If he could go back in time and not drink that moonberry juice, he would. There was no stopping what was about to happen though. Bait gave into it.

UUUUUUUUUUUURRRRRRRRRRRPPPPPPPP.

Ezran, Callum, and Rayla froze as the megaburp echoed through the canyon, as loud and menacing as a clap of thunder.

A moment later, an ice sheet broke free in the distance. It began slipping down the mountain, picking up speed and snow as it went.

"Avalanche!" Callum yelled. "Run!"

CHAPTER 25
SINKING HOPE

E zran scooped up Bait and they took off running, but Ezran's legs were too short to move through the deep powder very fast. He slipped and grabbed one of Rayla's hands to catch his balance, but she moaned and shook him off. Ezran noticed that her hand looked . . . purple?

"Oh my gosh," Ezran said. "What's happened to your hand?"

"Don't worry about it. Just run," Rayla said. With her good hand she yanked Ezran's arm and they continued down the path. But a few moments later, when she looked over her shoulder, Rayla knew the avalanche would overtake them.

"We're not going to make it," she said. "It's like a snow-nami."

Callum skidded to a stop on his heels and turned around to face the snow. Rayla was right—they could never outrun the avalanche. He had to do something. He reached into his bag.

"Callum, what are you doing?" Ezran asked, his voice full of fear.

"Get behind me," Callum said. "I have a plan."

Rayla, Ezran, and Bait obeyed.

Callum stepped forward and held the primal stone in front of him. He drew the wind breath rune in the air. The wall of white doom was only feet away.

"ASPIRO!" Callum yelled out into the storm. He blew with all the air he had in his lungs—a gust so strong that it split the snow, creating a sanctuary for the group. The avalanche rushed past them on both sides.

Callum blew and blew until he thought he would pass out. Finally, there was no more air left in his lungs. He inhaled, and snow pummeled into him, sweeping him off his feet.

Over and over he tumbled, careening down the mountain in a flurry of white, the primal stone tucked against his body. He finally came to a stop under several feet of snow.

He gasped for air as he pushed his way to the surface. It seemed the snow had settled peacefully on the mountain. But where were Rayla and Ezran?

"Is everyone okay?" Callum shouted into the eerie quiet. Then he saw Rayla's legs sticking out of the snow. A second later, she had kicked her way out of the drift and righted herself.

"I'm good," Rayla said, dusting some powder off her pants. "Where's that hiccupping, juice thief, frog-monster?" She held her hands out, ready to seize Bait by the neck.

Nearby, Bait popped up and shook the snow off himself.

"He's right behind you," Ezran said. "And he's okay." Ezran had landed on the icy surface of a frozen lake, yards away from everyone else. He looked himself up and down and determined he was still in one piece. "We're all okay!"

But the feeling of relief didn't last. Ezran checked his backpack—the egg was missing!

He twirled around in search of it. There it was—it had spun around on the ice and was lying a good ten feet away on the icy surface, glowing and unscathed but completely alone.

"I'll go get the egg," Ezran said. He stood up slowly and with great care made his way to the egg. He picked it up, but the extra weight of the egg was too much for the fragile ice. Small cracks started to form and multiplied quickly around his feet. Ezran froze clutching the egg, not knowing what to do.

"Ez! Don't move," Callum called to him from the shore. "We're coming to get you." He and Rayla slid down the snow to the edge of the lake. Callum crawled out onto the ice on all fours, trying to distribute his weight as evenly as possible, just like King Harrow had taught him on a winter holiday at the Banther Lodge years ago. "Stay still, we're almost there," he said. Rayla slid out onto the ice behind him.

As Callum approached Ezran, he reached his hands out for the egg.

"Easy does it. Just pass it over," he encouraged his brother.

Ezran carefully handed the egg to Callum.

But as Callum stood up with the extra weight of the egg,

cracks formed in the ice beneath him. He turned to Rayla, who was much closer to the shore.

"What now?" Rayla asked. It was as clear to her as it was to Callum that if they were going to get the egg safely off this fragile ice, Rayla would need to be part of the relay.

"Rayla, I'm going to hand you the egg. I'm sorry if I was a jerk before," Callum said. "We're lucky to have you as our friend. I do trust you." He held the egg out to Rayla like a peace offering, with a warm, trusting look in his eyes.

But Rayla shook her head as guilt welled up inside her.

"No, don't give me the egg," she said. "I don't deserve your trust, not yet. I need to tell you the truth." She closed her eyes. "This morning, the big rush was because I was attacked by someone. It . . . it was a human who was following us. I think he was sent by your aunt Amaya. I fought him off, but it was hard . . . because of this." She held up her injured hand and pointed to the tight ribbon constricting her wrist.

"This is an assassin's binding. A Moonshadow elf ritual. Before I met you, I swore an oath—I bound myself to end Prince Ezran's life. And this binding will never come off while he's alive. It will just get tighter and tighter until I lose my hand." Rayla looked at the princes. "But I'm ready to pay that price."

Ezran caught Rayla's eye. She'd lose her hand for him?

"Thank you for telling us," Callum said. "But we need to focus on the situation." He started to hand her the egg but Rayla took another deep breath and held up her hand.

"There's one more thing. The night I met you, something bad happened—"

CRACK! The ice beneath Callum split.

"Rayla, there's no time right now."

"Callum, I need to tell you—the king—!"

But the cracks were spreading rapidly in every direction.

"Just take it!" Callum pleaded. He shoved the egg into Rayla's arms.

Rayla was caught off guard, and though she tried to catch the egg, it was too heavy for her injured hand. It escaped her grasp, hit the ice, and broke through.

Callum's jaw dropped. There was now a huge hole in the ice, opening to the cold, black water beneath. The light of the egg faded and then disappeared as it sank in the deep water.

"You dropped it," he said to Rayla.

"I *just* told you my hand was messed up," Rayla cried.

"Well, use the other hand," Callum said.

"Stop arguing!" Ezran said. "We have to do something."

But before Callum or Rayla could make another move, Ezran dove into the icy hole. He disappeared into the murky water.

"Ez, no! Ezran," Callum called out into the hole. "I'm going after him," he said to Rayla.

But Rayla grabbed his arm.

"Don't," she said. "He has to do this alone. He'll get it; he'll save the egg. We must believe in him. And we're going to need to be up here to pull him out."

Ezran hadn't thought before diving into the freezing water. He wasn't sure if he had chosen his destiny or it had chosen him; he only knew that this was what he had to do.

But under the ice, the water was nearly pitch black. Ezran could barely see his hand in front of his face, let alone the egg. He paddled desperately in the direction he thought the egg had gone, scanning the dark for any sign of it. The cold pricked at his skin like daggers until numbness started to take over.

And then he saw something. It wasn't much—a glint of blue. His lungs burned as he pushed through the water, but the speck of light seemed to bob farther out of reach.

Then a strange sensation crept over Ezran's body. Warmth traveled from his toes to the top of his head. His mind went fuzzy.

But there—a bright light seemed to be getting closer. Without really trying, he drifted toward the white glow. The light started to take shape and a silhouette emerged. A sense of comfort washed over him—it must be his mother, he thought, here to retrieve him from the frozen waters. He did not remember her, but somehow he knew her. She smiled and beckoned Ezran toward the light. He paddled to reach her, and as he came closer, she appeared ready to hold him in her warm embrace. Ezran held his arms out in a circle to hug her.

But the moment Ezran wrapped his arms around the glow, he knew something was off. He wasn't hugging his mother; he was holding something hard and cold—it was the dragon egg!

Jolted out of his dreamy stupor, Ezran thrashed his legs to propel himself and the egg to the surface. But where was the hole he'd fallen through? He searched left and right but it was too late—his head hit ice. With one fist, he whacked on the ice above him, pounding as hard as he could.

Above the ice, Callum and Rayla waited in silence for Ezran to reemerge.

"Come on, come on..." Callum muttered. He thought he might throw up.

"It's going to be okay," Rayla said. "Ez will get it."

One minute passed, then two. Callum couldn't believe this was happening. He spun around toward Rayla.

"You were wrong, Rayla," Callum said. "He's not coming back."

Tears formed in Rayla's eyes as she accepted that Callum was probably right. "I'm so sorry, I thought he would be able to do this. I thought it was the way it had to be." She brought her hands to her face to wipe away the tears, her injured hand feeling extra cold.

Wait. Her binding.

"Callum, he's alive! Ezran has to be alive. Look at my binding. It's still tight." She looked around the ice frantically.

TAP! TAP! TAP!

In a flash, Rayla skidded over to Ezran, lay down, and used her blades to bash a hole in the ice. She dragged Ezran to the surface, struggling with the weight of his soaked clothing and the egg.

Callum grabbed Rayla by the ankles and pulled both her and Ezran back to shore, trying to ignore Ezran's bluish skin. Once on land, he wrapped his arms around his brother to generate some warmth. The egg rolled out of Ezran's grasp.

"Ezran. Ezran! You saved it, you got the egg back! You did it," Callum said.

There was no response.

He placed the back of his hand on Ezran's ice-cold cheek. "Please, Ezran, you've got to be okay! Just say something—speak to me."

Finally, finally, Ezran blinked his eyes open.

"I think I got a case of the frozey toe-sies," he said.

Callum hugged him tight and kissed him on the forehead. Rayla hugged both princes and everyone laughed with relief.

Then Ezran looked over at the egg, lying on its side nearby. "Oh no," he said. The egg's bright glow had dimmed to a flicker. "There's something wrong with the egg."

CHAPTER 26
THE DAGGER AND THE DOCTOR

E z, you should really try to sleep," Callum said.

Ezran sat close to the campfire, straining to stay awake. His teeth chattered and his whole body shivered, but he refused to rest because he wanted to watch over the ailing dragon egg. He wrinkled his nose, scrunched up his face, and sneezed. "I'm fide," he said through his stuffy sinuses.

Rayla and Callum had dragged a half-frozen Ezran and the egg up the mountain, where they located a small cavern that would protect them from the elements. Rayla built a fire and placed the egg nearby to warm it, then she left in search of food. Callum had his sketchbook on his knees and was drawing intently, but every few minutes he shot worried glances in the direction of Ezran and the egg.

"You're not *fide*," Callum said. "You need rest."

But instead of lying down, Ezran shuffled closer to Callum.

"What are you drawing?" he asked, leaning over Callum's shoulder to look. Callum braced himself for his brother's reaction.

"Oh . . ." was all Ezran said.

Callum thought he'd captured their mother's serenity and kindness pretty well. She was dressed in her crown and royal robes, with her hands clasped in front of her.

"When you were down there, under the ice, I was so scared," Callum said to his brother. "I thought I was going to lose you like we lost her." He tapped the drawing. "But somehow, you made it. And now I can't stop thinking . . . maybe she was watching over us." Callum knew it was his responsibility to talk to Ezran about their mother's death, to help him get through it, since he was the older brother. But so often, the subject was simply too difficult to broach.

"I miss her," Ezran said.

"If she knew what we were trying to do, she'd be proud of us," Callum said. Then he shook his head at Ezran. "And she would yell at you to go sit closer to the fire and bundle up," he added.

"I doe," Ezran said. He moved closer to the fire and warmed his hands.

"Oh, she's beautiful," Rayla said. She had entered the cave quietly and was admiring the drawing of Queen Sarai. "Is that your mother?"

Callum nodded.

Rayla didn't know what else to say, so she changed the

subject. "Um, I found some moonberries. I already picked out the poison ones." She placed a sack on the ground with her good hand, then unwrapped it with her injured hand, wincing. A small bunch of red berries rolled to the edges of the cloth. "This should keep us full for a day," she said.

While the boys gobbled some berries, Rayla examined the dragon egg, which was wrapped in cloth near the fire.

"It's even dimmer than when I left," Rayla said.

Ezran nodded. "We gotta fide help."

They looked at one another in silent agreement.

"That's what we'll do first thing in the morning," Rayla said. "Right now, the best thing we can do is sleep."

The next morning, Ezran's cold had improved significantly and he couldn't wait to get moving. He was the first one awake, so he put out the fire, cleaned the camp, and gingerly wrapped the egg in his pack. Then he woke up Callum and Rayla.

"Guys, let's go," he said. He hurried into the snow without waiting for a response. Callum and Rayla scrambled out after him, rubbing the sleep from their eyes.

It wasn't long before they came to a mountain village. The small, quaint houses were covered in at least a foot of snow, and smoke rose from the chimneys. A towering mountain with a flat top created a backdrop for the town.

"I knew I saw smoke!" Rayla said. "Maybe we can find help."

"Okay, sure. We might find a dragon egg expert," Callum said.

"But we will definitely find a bunch of elf-hating humans. And that's a problem."

"Or maybe it's not a problem," Rayla said. She had an idea. She ran over to Ezran's pack and grabbed his cloak. Then she turned away from the princes. "Get ready to meet"—she draped the garment over herself, making sure the hood covered her horns and pointy ears, then twirled around in the snow like a magician—"human Rayla!"

The boys didn't seem convinced.

"Just wait," Rayla said. "Once I pair my 'disguise' with my perfect human impression, the illusion will be complete." She stepped back and puffed up her chest.

"Greetings, fellow humans—human fellows." She spoke in a high-pitched, nasal accent. As she passed the boys, she elbowed Callum in the ribs and clapped Ezran on the back so hard he lost his balance. "I sure do like hanging out with other humans and talking about things like money and starting wars."

"That's pretty good," Ezran said.

"Totally, my good human friend," Rayla said. "Bring it in for a high four!" She raised her good, four-fingered elf hand up in the air and Ezran slapped it.

"Uhhhh . . . can you impersonate a fifth finger?" Callum asked.

"Right, right. I need some kind of a . . . hand disguise," Rayla said. She pondered her options. As luck would have it, someone had formed a mound of snow into the shape of a person. It was wearing gloves on its stick-arms.

"Look, guys! Snow elf," Rayla said, sprinting over to it.

"I'm pretty sure that's a snowman," Ezran said.

Rayla relieved the snowman of its gloves and pulled them on her own hands. She wiggled them in Callum's face. "Hand disguise," she said.

Callum poked the empty pinky finger and it bent backward. "Good enough, I guess. Just don't shake hands with anyone."

The trio (and Bait) headed toward the center of town despite Callum's worries about attracting too much attention. They came across a large crowd that had formed near an old stone fountain. A slender young man was standing on the edge of the fountain talking loudly to the group. He appeared to be putting on some sort of show and repeatedly pointed to a sheathed dagger on his belt. He waved his arms in the air theatrically. Callum and the others moved closer to hear what was going on.

"I defended the border against all manner of horrors and monstrosities—things you can't even imagine! There's nothing I, Tristan, fear now," the man said. He strutted around the fountain, fluffing up his fur collar and smoothing down his mustache. Then he held up a gloved finger as if suddenly stricken by an idea. He swiped a pouch from his belt and threw it down. Coins jingled within. "In fact, I wager I could defeat any challenger here with nothing but my dagger." He patted the small sheath on his hip.

The crowd broke into chatters. The man was obviously a conceited mercenary, but no one really wanted to take him on.

Soren would be all over this if he were here, Callum thought.

"Anyone dare to challenge me?" Tristan taunted.

Just then, a shadow fell over the performer as an enormous man in full armor stepped forward. He unsheathed an immense weapon and cackled. "This isn't even my biggest sword," he said.

The crowd whispered again, this time with excitement. A matronly lady whipped out a coin purse and shouted, "I'll take that bet!" Next to her a man called out, "My money on the big guy."

The giant and the mercenary squared off and Callum recognized an opportunity. "Everyone's distracted," he said. "Let's go."

But Rayla had noticed something about the mercenary's blade. She grabbed Callum's arm. "Check out the elven runes along the dagger's sheath."

The giant swung his sword as Tristan pulled the dagger out of its sheath. As Rayla has suspected, the blade was only a few inches long, but it glowed fiery orange as though it had just been pulled from the heat of a forge.

The magic dagger sliced through the giant's sword like butter and the broken half clanged to the ground. The hulk stared at the hilt of his sword, utterly dumbfounded, then dropped it and backed away in fear.

"Anyone else?" Tristan asked.

The crowd gasped in awe as Tristan scuttled around to pocket his winnings.

"What was that?" Callum asked over the din of the crowd.

"It's a Sunforge blade," Rayla said.

"Wow, I can't believe I just saw a real Sunforge blade," Ezran said. He paused. "What's a Sunforge blade?"

A little blip of excitement bubbled up in Rayla. "In Xadia, Sunfire elves can make magic weapons that stay as hot as the moment they're forged for hundreds of years," Rayla explained. She pointed to the runed sheath at the mercenary's belt. "See that? The sheath is inscribed with special runes to protect him from the heat. Otherwise, well . . ."

"His pants would be on fire?" Ezran asked.

"Yeah. His legs too," Rayla said.

Callum's eyes widened. "Rayla, if that blade can cut through a steel sword, would you say it can cut through pretty much anything?"

"Not just pretty much—it *can* cut through anything." Her eyes lit up as she heard her own words. "My wrist binding!"

Callum nodded. "You have to go get that dagger," he said. "Let's split up. Ezran and I will find help for the egg. You work on your binding. Then we'll meet back here at the fountain."

"But how will you get the dagger?" Ezran asked Rayla.

Rayla tugged up her hood and narrowed her eyes. "I'm going to ask nicely," she said.

The princes walked up and down the town streets until Ezran spotted a sign. It had the shapes of a cat and dog carved into it with a heart between the two animals.

"Look! Do you think this is some kind of animal doctor?" Ezran asked.

"I think so," Callum said. "Or . . . a dating service for pets."

Ezran gave Callum a look. "Probably an animal doctor."

"Yeah," Callum said.

"But that's a good idea!" Ezran added.

They pushed open the door and stepped inside. A bunch of stalls were occupied by farm animals with all sorts of ailments. Ezran saw a pig with pink eye, a cat with a broken tail, and a cow that appeared to have some sort of fungal infection on both its ears. An older man stood in front of a whinnying horse, tending to its rib cage.

"Be right with you," the doctor called without looking away from the horse. When he seemed satisfied the horse was okay, he walked toward the princes. But he jumped back when he caught sight of Bait.

"I'm so sorry," he said as he regained his composure. "There's nothing I can do for that poor creature."

Ezran looked at Bait. He was scowling like always but otherwise seemed fine.

"What?" Callum said. "Oh, no, no, he's fine. We have, uh, a different problem. Ez, tell him."

But now Ezran was distracted by the frazzled horse. The creature trembled, eyes wide and askew. "What happened to you, little sweetie?" he asked. The horse whinnied in response. "Aw, you saw something really scary, didn't you?"

The doctor turned back to the horse and put a bucket of feed in front of it. "She sure did. This one ran away up the Cursed Caldera. Whatever she saw, she's lucky it only scared her. Won't make that mistake again." He patted the horse kindly.

Meanwhile, Callum was petting an especially affectionate cat. "I see you've met Button Nose," said the doctor.

"Oh, is she called that because her nose is so cute and sweet, like a little button?" Callum asked. But before the doctor could answer, the cat turned around and slowly pushed her bottom into Callum's face.

The doctor explained, "She's actually named that because of how she places her posterior on the noses of people she likes. Guess she likes you!" Then the doctor turned to business. "So, what can I help you with?"

Callum suddenly realized he and Ezran hadn't discussed a plan. They couldn't talk about the dragon egg directly; they'd have to improvise.

"Well ... a friend of ours has a problem," Callum began. He looked to Ezran to pick up the bluff where he left off.

"Jofus," Ezran continued.

"Your friend's name is Jofus?" the doctor asked. He motioned for the boys to sit down at a long table on the other side of the barn.

"It's a real name," Ezran said.

"Err ... yes. Our friend Jofus has an egg," Callum continued. "An animal egg. He's been taking really good care of it. Keeping it warm, and safe ... wrapped in blankets ..." Then he said the last part really fast. "Except one time he dropped it into an icy lake for several minutes. Anywho."

"Sorry, what was that?" the doctor asked.

"HE DROPPED IT INTO AN ICY LAKE," Ezran repeated, slowly and loudly. He narrowed his eyes at Callum.

"Yeah. Jofus dropped it," Callum said. "It was Joe. Jofus."

"Right, of course. That sounds bad," the doctor said, clearly confused.

"Yeah. We're worried it's hurt. The egg is colder, and it doesn't glow like it used to," Callum said.

"Wait—a glowing egg?" The doctor ran a hand over his head and sighed. "Look, I can tell you have a real problem. I want to help, but I won't be able to unless you tell me what's really going on." He placed his hand over his heart. "I promise you, I'm not going to get you in trouble."

Callum and Ezran shared a look.

"You can't tell anyone," Ezran said.

"I won't. Okay? But you need to trust me," the doctor replied.

Callum took a deep breath and nodded, and Ezran slipped his backpack from his shoulders. He pulled back the flap and revealed the dragon egg. The doctor gasped.

"That's a dragon egg, isn't it?"

The princes nodded.

The doctor placed his hand gingerly onto the egg, stroking the fragile, precious treasure. "I've never seen one before, only pictures in books. But I'll do what I can."

Callum and Ezran held their breath as he began to examine the egg. He placed his ear against the dimly glowing shell and listened. He tapped it gently in a few different places and moved his hands over its surface. His brow furrowed and he muttered to himself. Finally, he looked up at the boys.

"Well, I do hear a heartbeat," he said.

Both boys let out a sigh of relief.

"That's good, right?" Ezran asked.

"But it's faint and slow. I'm afraid the egg is dying," the doctor said. "I don't know what I can do to save it. I'm so sorry."

Callum saw tears well up in Ezran's eyes, and a lump formed in his own throat.

"No. There has to be something you can do," Ezran said, hugging the egg. "Anything! Please."

Callum put a hand on his shoulder. "Come on, Ez, let's go. We'll find another way."

He helped Ezran put the egg into his backpack and then guided him toward the door.

They were halfway out when the doctor said, "Wait." The princes looked back.

"I'm hesitant to tell you about this, because it might be incredibly dangerous, but a dragon egg is so special it might be worth the risk. There was a miracle that happened a few years ago."

"A miracle?" Ezran repeated.

"But it happened on the Cursed Caldera," the doctor said. It looked like he was still considering whether he should tell the boys. Finally, he said, "There's someone I think you two should meet."

CHAPTER 27
SOMETHING PERSONAL
AND GROSS

Soren paced back and forth on the stone bridge that arched over the river, while Claudia sat with her head in her hands as if fighting off a pounding headache. "What are we going to do?" Soren asked. "What are we going to do? What are we going to do?"

They had arrived at the Banther Lodge not long ago with a pack of the finest tracking hounds in Katolis. Soren provided one of Callum's muddy training shirts for scent and directed the dogs on the trail of the princes. The hounds had run like mad toward the river . . . and then promptly lost the trail.

"Can you just be quiet for a minute? I'm trying to think," Claudia said. Her brother's incessant worrying was not helping.

"Every minute we sit here, the step-prince and the crown runt get farther and farther away," Soren snipped.

Claudia did have one idea. "I know a tracking spell that could locate them," she said. "But first I need something from the princes."

"We have this," Soren said, whipping out Callum's training shirt.

"Nooo," Claudia said, smacking her palm on her forehead. "Something more personal than a shirt."

"You mean like underwear?" Soren asked.

"Ew, gross." Claudia made a face. "I mean like spit, or toenails."

Soren huffed. "We don't have time to search the whole lodge for toenails, Claudia," he said, throwing up his arms. "We have to figure this out. If I fail, I don't know what Dad will do to me. And I'm already failing at step one—I mean, never mind."

"Never mind what?" Claudia asked.

But Soren brushed past Claudia with a look of importance on his face. He walked purposefully toward a tree some twenty yards behind her and pointed to an arrow stuck in the bark.

Claudia followed him—there was a woven plait of silvery hair flapping softly in the wind, pinned by the arrow.

Soren yanked the arrow from the tree and held it up. "You said something like spit or toenails. What about elf hair?"

"Yes, it's perfect," Claudia said, caressing the braid. "We'll find Callum and Ezran wherever we find that vile bloodthirsty elven assassin."

She examined the silver hair for another moment.

"Cute braid, though!"

○

Back in the mountain village, the mercenary Tristan strutted down the street jingling the bag of his winnings. This was the most gold he'd had in months. But halfway to the corner, he stopped.

Was he being paranoid, or had he heard something? He glanced over his shoulder, but the street was empty. Then, out of the corner of his eye, he caught a flash of someone behind him. He shoved the gold into his pocket.

"I won this money fair and square," he shouted into the empty street.

When no one responded, Tristan took a sudden left turn and darted down an alleyway. He ran hard, turning corners and hopping fences. Eventually, he skidded to a stop at a dead end, breathing hard.

Rayla, on the other hand, had barely broken a sweat, and now the mercenary was right where she wanted him. She dropped down from her spot on the roof, landing in front of Tristan.

"I don't want your money," Rayla said from beneath her cloak.

"Then what do you want from me?" Tristan asked. The poor thing looked terrified.

Rayla held up her hands in surrender. "I just want your help," she said. "Seriously, I don't want to fight you. I just want to borrow your blade to cut this." She pushed her glove down her arm just far enough to show the white binding digging deep into her wrist, the bruising obvious against her pale skin.

"Oh, you just want to 'borrow' it," Tristan said. "Do you know how valuable this blade is?"

"Fine," Rayla said. She was getting tired of no one trusting her. "You hold the blade. Just try to cut this ribbon off me."

"But it'll burn you," Tristan said, peering more closely at the binding.

"I don't care! Just do it—please," Rayla pleaded.

Tristan shrugged and unsheathed his dagger. Rayla could see the heat radiating off the glowing steel and she winced as the dagger got closer to her arm. But before the blade could even touch the binding, her glove started smoking and went up in flames.

"OWWW!" Rayla yelped. She tore off the glove and stomped on it to put out the fire.

But once the fire was out, Rayla realized her mistake. Tristan was staring at her in terror. More specifically, he was staring at her four-fingered elf hand in terror.

"You're one of them," Tristan said. He took a few steps backward.

Rayla donned her best human impression. "Who me? I'm just a simple human girl who likes the human things. Like bread. And complaining all the time," she said. She put on her sweetest smile and twirled a lock of her white hair.

"No," Tristan said. "I know what you are—you're an elf." He raised his blade.

Rayla knew the game was up. "Fine, I'm an elf," she said. Then she grabbed Tristan's wrist, twisted it behind his back, and disarmed him. He staggered away, weaponless and horrified.

"Calm down, this will only take a second," Rayla said. She picked up the dagger and brought it as close to the binding as she could bear, then closed her eyes, gritted her teeth, and went in for the slice. "ARRGGG!" she cried as blistering heat scorched her skin. Had it worked?

She opened her eyes. The binding was as tight as ever. "No! Nothing can cut this stupid binding!" she said.

Tristan kneeled at Rayla's outburst and begged for her mercy. "Please, just take the dagger. Don't hurt me," he cried.

Rayla sighed. "I'm not going to hurt you. And I'm not going to steal from you either," she said.

She tossed the dagger to the ground and walked away.

CHAPTER 28
ELLIS AND AVA

Callum and Ezran knocked on the door of a snow-covered cabin nestled deep in the woods. The animal doctor had told them to find the cabin if they wanted to learn about a mysterious miracle healer.

A young girl opened the door a crack and blinked at the princes with wondering eyes. She was wearing a hat, boots, and a heavy winter coat. Her long black hair hung in a single braid down her back.

Then an animal's snout pushed through the door and Callum and Ezran found themselves face-to-face with a full-grown wolf—a very big wolf. Sitting down, it was taller than the girl was standing up. The wolf sniffed both princes and then nodded approvingly.

"Hi," the girl said. "I'm Ellis. And this is my sweetie-wolf, Ava." Ellis ruffled the fur on Ava's head. "How can I help you?"

"Hi, I'm Callum and this is Ezran," Callum said. "The animal doctor sent us to you. He said you would know something about a miracle healer..." He trailed off, realizing that his request might sound a little strange. But Ellis didn't bat an eye.

"The doctor's right," she said. "There was a miracle. I still don't really understand how it happened. But I do know this— without it, Ava would be dead."

Callum and Ezran looked at each other. Maybe this little girl was going to help them save the egg after all.

"Why don't you come in?" Ellis asked. She opened the door and led the princes toward a roaring fireplace in the cabin's great room. Callum and Ezran warmed themselves by the hearth as Ellis settled into a nearby chair. Ava padded over and Ellis scratched the wolf's neck. A shiny stone dangled from her collar.

"Please tell us your story," Ezran said.

Ellis smiled and settled deeper into her chair. It had been a while since anyone had wanted to hear it. "Well, two years ago, I found Ava in the woods. She was just a little cub and the cutest thing I'd ever seen. Somehow, she'd gotten herself caught in a rusty hunter's trap and her front paw was crushed. She was absolutely terrified." She stroked Ava's ears and the wolf let out a contented sigh. "She didn't want any help at first, but I could tell she had a determined spirit. When she finally let me unlock the trap, I took her to the animal doctor, the one who sent you here."

Ezran smiled. He liked Ellis already.

"The doctor said her leg was bad—so bad it had to be removed," Ellis continued. "When the operation was over, I named her Ava and took her home to heal. She was hopping around on three legs in no time."

Ava wagged her tail. She remembered those days fondly—the gentleness with which Ellis changed her bandages, and the way Ellis snuggled up to her at night, like her own mother used to.

"But Ava wasn't welcomed by my father," Ellis went on, a sadness creeping across her face. "He said there was only suffering in her future. He said . . ." Ellis trailed off. It was hard to say even now. "He wanted to put her down."

Ezran shuddered. He understood not wanting animals to suffer, but putting an animal down just because they were missing a leg? It wasn't fair. It wasn't just.

Ellis regained her composure and continued. "I knew Ava would become strong and healthy if given the chance. I scooped her up and ran. The only safe place would be where no one would follow us, so we started up the Cursed Caldera."

"What's the Cursed Caldera?" Callum asked, though he was afraid to hear the answer.

"It's the mountain where only monsters find their refuge," Ellis said. "At least, that's what the legends say, and Ava and I found it to be true." Ava whimpered but Ellis went on. "A blizzard made it hard to see much in front of us, but strange shapes and terrifying eyes seemed to pop out through the wind and snow. The higher we climbed, the more terrifying creatures lurked in the shadows. We kept going though. We found an ancient tree with a hollow trunk and huddled inside. That's when she appeared."

"Who?" Ezran asked. He'd made himself comfortable on the floor and was now stroking Ava's ears.

"I still don't know," Ellis said. "We couldn't see her face—only her silhouette against the full moon. But she's the reason Ava is here. She cradled her in her arms, called her beautiful and perfect. And then this white light came from her hands. It was so bright, I had to shield my eyes." Ellis put an arm up over her face as if blocking the sun, then took it down again. "And when she handed Ava back to me—I couldn't believe it. Ava's fourth leg was completely healed. This Moonstone collar had appeared around her neck too." She reached down and scratched Ava under her collar. The wolf yelped as if to say "The end."

The princes were speechless but looked at each other with newfound excitement.

"We have to find this miracle healer," Callum said. "If she can save a cub's missing paw . . ."

"Maybe she can save a dragon egg," Ezran said. Then he clapped his hands over his mouth.

"Wait, a what?" Ellis asked.

"Uhhh," Callum started. "He said, 'Maybe she can shave a wagon leg.'"

Ellis tried to ask more questions, but the princes had already stood up and put on their cloaks.

"Uh, sorry," Ezran said. "We have to go."

"Thank you so much, Ellis," Callum said as they made their way to the door.

And then it was just Ellis and Ava in the cabin again, the fire crackling in the hearth.

Rayla pulled her hood close around her face while she waited by the fountain for the boys. There was a chill in the air already; it would be another cold night.

"Did you find the knife guy? Did you get his knife?" Ezran suddenly appeared, running up to Rayla with a huge smile on his face. Callum was right behind him.

Rayla held up her wrist. "The bad news is that the Sunforge blade didn't work," she said. She breathed deeply for dramatic effect. "The good news is the binding will fall off naturally . . . when my hand does."

Callum winced. "Ugh, Rayla, I'm sorry to hear that."

"It's fine," Rayla said. "Just give me some good news. Tell me something good happened with the egg."

"Yes and no. Well, no," Callum stammered. "Not yet, but maybe! So yes? In a way."

"Okay, that's averaging out to around a 'maybe-minus,'" Rayla said.

"Yeah, that's about right," Callum agreed.

"We learned about a miracle healer," Ezran said. "Someone who might be able to help the egg. And maybe your hand too!"

Ezran's enthusiasm was contagious. Rayla felt a glimmer of excitement. "Really?" she asked. "A miracle healer?"

"The only catch is that the healer lives up there," Callum said. He pointed to an ominous flat-topped mountain in the distance. "It's called 'the Cursed Caldera.'"

Rayla hung her head. "Please tell me the mountain's named that because it was discovered by the great explorer, Sir Phinneas Kirst."

"Well, no," Callum started to explain. "It's apparently infested with horrible monsters—"

"Yeah, no, I know," Rayla said. It was worth asking.

Suddenly, they heard shouting and clanging heading in their direction. A familiar voice shouted, "There she is!" and Rayla's eyes widened in fear. Tristan came running from around the corner leading a pack of angry villagers.

"She's an elf!" Tristan yelled.

Rayla jumped up and covered herself with her cloak. "Oh, right, I forgot about the other bad news," she said to the princes. "Let's move!"

She sprinted away from the violent, elf-fearing humans with Ezran and Callum following behind. The crowd chased the gang over bridges, through narrow passages, and all the way to the edge of the village, swords and pitchforks ready to slaughter an enemy.

"Suddenly, the Cursed Caldera doesn't seem like such a bad option," Rayla yelled over her shoulder.

And so they fled toward the caldera, where black winds

swirled wildly around a volcanic-shaped peak. They ran through snow and mist, barely noticing the darkening sky.

Finally, gasping in the thinning air, the group collapsed at the base of a tree and looked down the mountain for their pursuers. No one was coming; they were entirely alone on the caldera.

"I think we're safe," Callum said.

The forest stretched around them in all directions, and the path upward loomed darker than where they had come from. Mysterious sounds echoed all around.

"Guys, this place is pretty creepy," Ezran said. Bait grunted his assent.

"Safe. Sure," Rayla said. "So how are we supposed to find this miracle healer? And what's that?"

She pointed to a rock just above them.

A large, shadowy creature stood looking down on them with glimmering green eyes. The beast pawed at the ground, snarling under its breath. Rayla put one hand on a blade, but then, the last of the fading daylight illuminated the creature.

Ezran smiled. It wasn't one creature—it was two.

"Come with me," Ellis said from atop Ava's back. "I'll help you find the healer." She yanked on Ava's collar and the wolf bounded up the rocks.

CHAPTER 29
THE CURSED CALDERA

"So...what, exactly, are we doing here?" Soren asked Claudia.

She had hopped on her horse back at the Banther Lodge and taken off without a single word. Now they were miles away at the base of a steep cliff. This was a place her mother had taken her so many years ago to show her something beautiful. A few years after that, her father had brought her here to show her something practical.

Claudia was on her hands and knees, gathering something from the base of the cliff wall. Soren waited, arms crossed, feeling out of place.

Claudia stood up. "I just need one more thing for the tracking spell. Then we can find the princes and complete our mission."

She walked away from Soren, tracing her hand along the edge of the mountain.

"Special rocks? Magic twig?" Soren asked. Her silence was beyond irritating. Soren recognized that Claudia's magic was useful, but he found ingredient-hunting for spells extremely tedious.

"Ah, here it is!" she finally said. Claudia slipped through an opening on the side of the cliff and beckoned for Soren to follow. "This way."

Soren sprinted after his sister but came to a grinding halt when he saw the size of the opening. "You're kidding, right?" he said. The crevice was barely large enough for any human adult, let alone one wearing armor. He groaned as he contorted his body to squeeze through the tiny opening. "If only...I weren't...so muscular," he said, barely managing to pass through.

Claudia led the way through the damp, narrow cave, her palm glowing with magic light. She glided easily around the rocky twists and turns of the passage while Soren bumped off one side of the cave to the other, his armor clanging.

"This is why I hate magic," Soren said. "It always involves something really creepy." He ran his hand along the wall to steady himself but stopped when he touched something sticky. A black, gooey substance covered his palm. When he tried to wipe off the tar-like sludge on a different rock he ended up getting cobwebs stuck to his hand. "This is so gross."

But Claudia wasn't paying any attention to Soren. She was

fully absorbed in her task, flicking the light into all the cave's crevices.

"Where is it ...?" she muttered to herself. Claudia was beginning to feel frustrated. It was the first time she had come here without guidance. And both her parents had known their way around so well, they could literally find the secret place in the dark. "Wait! I know how to find it." She closed her hand, snuffing out the light.

"Ack. Claudia, what are you doing?" Soren asked. "I can't see a thing."

"Shh ..." Claudia said.

"Oh, can you see better if I'm quiet?" Soren asked.

Claudia gave Soren a sisterly smack on the shoulder. "Give it a moment. Let your eyes adjust."

Soren decided to humor his sister and stood quietly. After an uncomfortable minute in pitch darkness, he saw a subtle glow up ahead of them.

"Look. There it is," Claudia whispered. She began walking toward the light.

Soren followed Claudia around a corner and without warning, the oppressive cavern walls gave way into a spacious, sparkling grotto.

Soren gasped. Lush trees filled the deep underground space. A stream ran over the tangled roots and mossy stones beneath them. And there were twinkling, floating things flitting around the air, each casting a soft white glow. Soren had never seen anything like it.

"These are called wisps," Claudia said, pulling a jar out of her bag. "Still think magic is creepy and gross?"

Soren was too awestruck to respond.

Claudia captured a few of the magical wisps as if she were catching fireflies on a summer night. Then she closed the jar and held it up to Soren.

"All right, so what else do we need for this spell?" Soren asked.

"Nothing. We're all set," Claudia said.

"Really? Great," Soren said. That hadn't been so bad after all.

"We just have to climb to the top of the tallest mountain in Katolis," Claudia said with a smile.

"That's what I'm talking about!" Soren responded, excited for the challenge.

"It's a fun spell," Claudia said.

○

Rayla walked alongside the giant wolf and small girl, feeling skeptical about the addition to the group. She was used to being the most informed member and didn't appreciate being led up a cursed mountain by a small child.

"So, hi there," Rayla said, trying her best to keep her tone friendly. She waved her hand at the girl. "And, who are you, exactly?"

"Me? I'm Ellis," the girl said in her chipper voice. "And this is Ava. She's a wolf." Ellis patted Ava and smiled at Rayla.

"Wolf? You don't say," Rayla replied. "I thought she might be a bird."

Ava wasn't sure if the elf was serious, so she gave her a huge sloppy kiss on the side of her face. That ought to prove she was a wolf.

Rayla cringed.

A few yards ahead of them, Callum turned around. "Oh, I should have introduced you guys." He had avoided introductions thus far because he wasn't sure if Ellis's unbridled enthusiasm would mix well with Rayla's dry sarcasm, and it seemed he was right. But he'd put it off long enough. "Ellis, this is Rayla," Callum said. "We originally met because, well . . ." Callum scratched his head. There really was no delicate way to phrase the exceptional beginnings of their relationship with Rayla. So he spoke quickly, with as much cheerfulness as he could. "She broke into our castle on a mission to kill Ezran."

Rayla looked at Ellis with a sheepish smile and shrugged.

"But it doesn't matter," Ezran added. "We're past all that now." He waved his hand as if to brush off this old news. Ellis took the cue.

"People meet in so many interesting ways," she squeaked.

Rayla still wasn't sure she trusted this Ellis, but she appreciated a human who didn't seem to mind elves. "Well, now that we've completed the introductions, how do we find this healer?" she asked.

"Truth is, I never found her—she found us," Ellis said. "We were hiding in a big, twisty, hollow tree, up near the rim." Ellis pointed to the peak.

"Then we need to get to that tree," Callum said. "Even if it takes all night."

"Wait a second," Rayla said, holding up her hands. "That's all we have to go on? A weird tree where this miracle worker showed up two years ago?"

"It's our only chance," Callum said. "Got a better idea?"

"As a matter of fact—" Rayla began. But she had nothing. "No."

Ava pranced by Callum and Rayla. "Now that we've settled that," Ellis called out, "I'll get us to that tree, the healer will find us there, and she'll save the egg."

"And maybe she can help your hand," Ezran said to Rayla.

"Don't worry about my hand," Rayla said, cradling her useless limb. "The egg is all that matters now."

And so, one foot in front of another, as the afternoon wore on, they climbed the Cursed Caldera. They jumped over ledges, climbed rickety fallen trees, and walked single file along narrow ridges, all sharing the weight of the heavy dragon egg. The hours passed quickly as they navigated the many obstacles, and by the time they reached a clearing halfway up the mountain, the day was ending. Ellis and Ava rode out onto a jutting edge. The sun was low, and the sky was on fire with a blazing sunset.

"It's so beautiful. It's like the sky is painted with honey," Ellis said with a sigh.

"Wow," Ezran said, taking in the pinkish-orange twilight sky.

"Too bad it also means the nightmares are about to begin," Ellis said.

"What do you mean, 'the nightmares'?" Rayla asked.

"Oh, you know," Ellis said in a cheery voice, "enormous monsters and indescribable terrors, stuff like that."

"'Stuff like that,'" Callum echoed. Ellis had mentioned the monsters before, but he'd sort of forgotten about them, what with all the climbing and egg-carrying and such.

"Yeah! And the higher we go, the worse it will get," Ellis assured them.

"All right—well, let's go!" Rayla said, pumping a fist with mock enthusiasm.

"No, no wait," Callum said. "We're going to need a plan." He wasn't about to have a repeat of the river monster incident.

"How can you plan for indescribable terrors?" Ezran wanted to know. "I feel like you need to be able to describe them first."

"I can try to help with that," Ellis said. "I would call the terrors horrifying, bloodcurdling, and creepy. But creepy in a super extreme way that feels like it's lighting your soul on fire," she added.

"I think that helps," Ezran said, though his expression said otherwise. Bait didn't look convinced either.

Callum closed his eyes—he just needed a minute to think. They had defeated the river monster with teamwork; maybe they could do the same here. *Think, Callum, think*, he told himself. *Rayla's got her blades. I have two spells—well, one and a half. Ellis has Ava. Ezran has—*

"I think I've got something," he said, opening his eyes. He held up his hand to stop anyone from interrupting, then announced his plan with a flourish.

"Flash! Woof! Whoosh! Slish-slash," he said.

Ellis stared at Callum. What he'd said was nonsense, but he seemed very excited about it.

She shouted, "Awesome!" and gave Callum a thumbs-up. But then she leaned over to Rayla and whispered, "Um, is he okay?"

"I think he's finally cracked under the pressure," Rayla said.

"No, I haven't cracked," Callum said. "That's the name of the plan. Ezran, you have the first job. You hold Bait in the air so he can flash and blind whatever monster we encounter. That's 'Flash.'"

"Wait," Ezran said. "But then I'm not really doing anything, I'm just kind of holding up Bait?"

"You're support. Every team needs a great support," Callum said. Nothing would interfere with his plan. "Ellis, you're next. Ava will bark, and you'll ride around in circles, barking to confuse the monster. That's 'Woof.'"

"What do you think, Ava?" Ellis asked, giggling. "Do you think you can run around and bark a lot?"

Ava let out a series of happy barks.

"She's ready," Ellis declared.

"Then it's my turn," Callum said. "I'll use my wind-breath spell for 'Whoosh.'" He held up the primal stone and mimed casting a spell.

"You're going to use magic?" Ellis said, so excited she stood up on Ava's back.

"Oh, it's just a simple rune," Callum said. "Just this thing I picked up. No big deal."

"Yeah, he's going to blow on the monster," Rayla said. She wriggled her fingers in the air. "He'll ruffle its fur real good."

"Well, it's either that or the half of the lightning spell

I know," Callum said, taking offense. "Specifically, the half that doesn't shoot lightning out of my fingertips."

"That monster won't know what hit it," Ezran said to Callum, then gave him a pat on the back, like Callum often did to him. "Oh wait, it will know what hit it. It'll be wind."

Callum frowned, but there were bigger things to worry about than his little brother teasing him.

"Anyway," he said, "Rayla, you're last—you're the finisher. You'll take the blinded, distracted, windblown monster down with your blades—'Slish-slash.'" Callum swiped his arms in the air for effect.

"My hand is in pretty bad shape," Rayla said, waving her purple hand at Callum. "I'm only going to be able to use one blade."

"Okay, no problem. We'll revise." Callum said. "You're just 'Slash.'" He cut through the air with one of his arms.

"No way, that won't work," Rayla said, holding up her healthy hand. "The good one is my 'Slish' hand."

"Really?" Callum asked.

"No, not really, dummy." Sometimes, Rayla could barely believe the denseness she had to put up with. She was completing a monumental eye roll when she brightened with a novel idea. "Wait, Callum. You are a dummy, but you're not a fool," she said.

"Am I supposed to feel flattered by that comment?" Callum asked.

"You said Claudia called you a fool when you interrupted her lightning spell," Rayla said. "But I'll bet she was actually saying 'FUL-minis.' It's the Draconic word for lightning."

"So, if 'Fulminis' is the trigger word," Callum began.

"Then you know the spell for lightning!" Ezran finished.

Callum picked up his primal stone with confidence. "Revised plan, team," he said. "Flash! Woof! ZAP! Slash!"

He envisioned everyone putting their hands in the middle and chanting the plan together, but they all just turned and continued up the mountain.

All right, Callum thought. *Your loss.* Then he began the trek, the plan becoming his mantra with each step.

Flash-woof-zap-slash.

Flash-woof-zap-slash.

CHAPTER 30
WORSE THAN DEATH

Back in Katolis, Viren carried a golden tray full of Xadian delicacies down to the dungeon. He had previously tried in vain to persuade his elven captive to eat and drink. But no amount of coaxing or threats had convinced the elf to break his fast.

In the dungeon, the elven assassin was just as Viren had left him. His body dangled from the stone wall where his wrists had been locked with iron chains, his muscular shoulders straining at the weight. He kept his head down and his blue eyes closed in some sort of perpetual meditation. Viren stood over him, casting a shadow across the elf's body.

"Enough brooding, elf. My patience wears thin," Viren said. He knelt and set down the tray. The assassin opened his eyes but turned his face away when he saw the food.

"You know, if you don't eat, you'll die," Viren said.

"I am already dead," the elf replied.

"You don't look dead," Viren said. He allowed a false look of confusion to spread over his face. "Though I will say that hand has seen better days." He pointed to the assassin's left arm, which was still bound by the white ribbon. The hand was almost black.

"I went out of my way to acquire some rare Xadian fruits," Viren said. He plucked a lumpy, magenta, pear-shaped fruit from the tray and held it up to admire it. "They're remarkable. So strange and exotic. And these Xadian oranges—no seeds." Viren cut a slice of the orange and popped it in his mouth. "Incredible," he said. He held a slice out toward the elf, who didn't budge. "No? I understand the whole 'honor in not eating' thing, but at least drink something." Viren lifted a glass pitcher and poured red liquid into a matching goblet. "Don't worry, it's just berry juice," he said.

The elf glowered.

Viren sighed. He had little patience for these flowery games. He stood up and took a sip of the juice. "I'll cut to the chase," he said. "I have a simple proposition. I want you to look at an object and tell me what it does. If you tell me the truth, I will unchain you, and you can walk out of here. What I'm asking is painless and easy."

The assassin's only response was to close his eyes. Viren waited a few moments, then spoke sharply. "Decide, elf. You can be free, or you can sit here and die."

"I told you," the elf said. "I am already dead."

"Ah yes, wait a second, I think I have heard about this," Viren said as he collected the tray and walked toward the door. "It's a Moonshadow elf thing, right? A philosophy of accepting you are already dead, so you will not fear death." Viren smiled. "What a beautiful challenge you've given me. I must come up with something you will fear . . . more than death."

He slammed the dungeon door on his way out, leaving Runaan in the dark to guess what it was that could be worse than death.

○

The sun had set completely on the Cursed Caldera, and the sky was growing darker by the minute. Up high, the flora was scarce and the trees barren, and the forest floor had given way to a dusty, dried mud. Mist and clouds obscured the path, but Bait glowed softly in Ezran's arms, illuminating the way.

Callum walked cautiously, prepared for the nightmares Ellis had warned them of, but so far all was calm.

"Well, it's dark," he said. "But I think the scariest thing I've heard so far is this angry cricket." He bent over a rock to look at the chirping insect. "And he doesn't even sound that angry, more like mildly annoyed."

"Yeah . . . are you sure this is the Cursed Caldera?" Ezran asked. "Or did we accidentally go wandering up Humdrum Hill?" Everyone laughed nervously at Ezran's joke.

"Maybe we took a wrong turn and wound up on Sleepy Slope," Rayla said.

"I'll have to check my map," Callum said, eager to join in, "but I'm pretty sure I recognize the unmistakable topography of . . ." He paused, building anticipation for his punch line. "Mount Monotonous!"

Callum waited for his joke to hit, but the only response he got was the chirp of the irritated cricket. He made a mental note to work on his delivery.

"Moving on," Ellis said. "It *is* a little odd that nothing bad has happened yet." She looked up as the clouds over the moon started to clear. "Maybe we're just luck— Ahhh! There's a huge scary monster!" She pointed right behind Callum.

"Ahhhhh!" Callum screamed.

"But don't worry, it's dead," Ellis said.

"Then why did you say it like that?" Callum asked. His heart was all the way up in his throat.

"Say it like what?" Ellis asked in her upbeat squeal.

Callum shook his head. Somehow no matter what Ellis said, she always sounded excited.

Ava trotted over to the swampy bog area where the monster was, and the group followed. As the mist cleared and the full light of the moon shone down, they could see a massive creature sprawled across their path, flat and lifeless.

Ezran approached the creature.

"I've never seen anything like this," he said. The monster seemed like a cross between a lion and a rodent, but it was about the size of an elephant. "And look at those circles on its fur. They remind me of a target. What a strange birthmark." Ezran pointed at a circular pattern on the beast's abdomen and reached out to put his hand on its side.

"Don't touch it!" Callum yelled. "I don't think that's a birthmark. It's a bite mark."

Ezran examined the creature again. His brother had a point. This poor creature was the prey, which meant somewhere out there, an even bigger predator lurked.

"You're right," Rayla said to Callum. She gestured to the creature's unnaturally pale skin. "Something drained all its blood."

Sluuuuurrrp.

Callum froze. The noise had come from behind the dead monster.

"Guys," Ellis said, "I see a much huger, scarier monster. And this one's alive."

She pointed to a huge shadow rising through the mist, and suddenly, a colossal leech appeared. The faceless, fifty-foot bloodsucker reared up over them, teeth bared.

"Okay, I'm not feeling bored anymore," Ezran said.

The leech screeched at a painful pitch and everyone covered their ears.

"The plan! The plan," Callum called out. "Time for the plan. Ezran—go!"

"Okay, okay," Ezran said. He looked in his arms, where Bait had been sitting seconds ago. "Wait, where's Bait?"

Bait's ears perked up at the sound of his name. He'd been trying to catch the cricket. But if it was time for the plan, he'd have to abandon his snack aspirations; he had a duty to fulfill. He gathered up all his glow and let it flash free.

Everyone else tried to cover their eyes but it was too late; they were momentarily blinded.

"Too soon, too soon," Callum cried as he stumbled around.

Thwap! The colossal leech smacked down near Ava and Ellis. Ava took off but ran right into Ezran, who was on his knees, patting the ground in a blind search for Bait.

Callum's sight was starting to come back, but everything was still fuzzy. "What about the rest of the plan?" he shouted. "I probably shouldn't do lightning if I can't see, right?"

"Don't do the lightning," Rayla ordered.

"Maybe a new plan?" Ezran suggested.

"Scatter! Run!" Callum yelled as his vision finally recovered. He took off behind Ellis and Ava, the leech nipping at his heels.

"This way, Callum," Ellis said, reaching her hand down to him. "Ava will get us out of here."

Callum grabbed hold of Ellis's arm and lurched onto Ava's back. The wolf bounded through the trees, but the leech was surprisingly agile for its size and stayed right on their tail.

Callum had just about lost hope when Ava scrambled up a pile of rocks, leaving the leech below. It roared after them in frustration, then slithered off toward Rayla and Ezran.

Rayla used her good arm to snatch Ezran and Bait out of the way of the coming leech. "You can climb trees, right?" Rayla asked. Without waiting for a response, she pushed Ezran and Bait up onto the nearest branch and they scrambled to safety. Rayla used her good hand to stick her blade into the bark of the tree and flung herself into the leaves, coming up beside Ezran and Bait. From their perch high above, they stared down at the monster.

"What do we do now?" Rayla asked. "I think that thing is waiting for us at the bottom of the tree."

"We don't even have that much blood," Ezran noted.

"I know," Rayla said. Then she shouted at the monster, "We would be a very unsatisfying snack!"

The leech roared.

"I guess an unsatisfying snack is still a snack," she said.

Callum's voice suddenly rang out from the hillside. "We don't have a choice. We'll just have to wait it out. I'm sorry my plan was a mess."

"Nah, your plan was fine," Rayla called back. "Our execution was a little off."

⟲

Runaan did not know exactly how much time had passed since the high mage's last appearance in the dungeon, but it was not much; Viren was one of the most impatient humans the elf had ever encountered. The high mage entered the dungeon straining to push a covered object. He brought it to a stop in front of Runaan.

"In a moment, I will remove this cover and you will tell me what you know. Understood?" Viren said. He knelt down in front of Runaan and pulled out a pouch filled with coins, jingling it in his palm. "I've brought something I hope you will find motivating," he said.

Runaan scoffed at the leather pouch. "You're more foolish than I thought," he said. "Don't you know only humans can be bribed?"

"Oh, this isn't a bribe," Viren said, a single corner of his mouth turning upward. "It's more of a threat." He dumped two coins out and flicked them toward Runaan. "Go on, take a closer look."

Runaan glanced at the coins and then did a double-take. These were no ordinary coins. They were powerful, magical, and cursed. Runaan's heart twisted in pain when he saw the anguished faces captured on the surfaces of the coins, the faces of people he knew and loved. Brave elves whose disappearances had made no sense to him, until now. "You're a monster," he said to Viren.

"You're mistaken," the high mage said, his mouth twitching. "I'm a pragmatist." He ripped the cloth from the object he had wheeled in and revealed a large mirror with runes around its edges. "Tell me what you know about this relic or I will seal your fate."

Runaan shook his head in disbelief. This relic had one purpose—to protect the world from an ancient and mysterious threat. The high mage clearly didn't know what he had in his possession. "You have succeeded," Runaan said.

Viren brightened a little. "Oh, have I?" he asked.

"That mirror?" Runaan said. "You have found something worse than death."

"Then tell me," Viren said. He seemed barely able to contain himself. "What. Is. It?"

Runaan knew the human's threats were not idle, and the fate he was now facing was horrifying. For an instant, a tiny crack appeared in his sense of resolve. Runaan could endure any pain, but his beloved husband, Ethari... Runaan's disappearance would cause him immense anguish.

But when Runaan imagined Ethari's face, the cracks in his resolve were filled with hope and true courage. "I will never help you," Runaan said to Viren.

"Then you're of no use to me," the high mage replied. He picked up his staff and removed a black candle from his robes. Then he began to chant, his voice becoming breathy and otherworldly. "Erusaert ym si luos ruoy ..."

Runaan steadied himself for his fate, though he would not go without a fight.

As the high mage's chants grew faster and more intense, blue vapors trickled off Runaan's body toward Viren's staff. Runaan strained at his chains and let out a guttural roar.

Louder and louder Viren chanted, his spell seeming to vaporize Runaan's body from the inside out, sucking it toward the staff.

Runaan strained once more, a terrified scream escaping his mouth, but he was powerless against Viren's dark magic.

In the adjacent chamber, Gren could hear Viren chanting, soft and slow at first, then faster. At the same time, he heard the elf leader's throaty protests transform into shrill screams that wracked the dungeon walls. A purple light started to pulsate from the cell. Then all at once, the elf's yells went silent and the purple glow disappeared.

Gren's eyes went wide. Was this standard protocol for all the high mage's prisoners, or just elven assassins?

A moment later, Viren emerged from the elf's chamber. His eyes were black and hollow, and his skin was pale and ghastly. He looked almost demonic. Gren shivered.

The high mage stopped just inside Gren's chamber, still in his own world. He held up something small and shiny and examined it, an arrogant look on his face. Gren craned his neck to see what the object was, but the light in the dungeon was dim, and his chains only reached so far. Was it a button, perhaps, or a coin? The high mage rarely concerned himself with such ordinary things . . .

Viren had planned to hold off admiring his work until he was in his office, but patience was not his strong suit these days. He stared at the elf leader's tortured face, now engraved on the golden coin. It screamed and writhed silently from within, as if the elf were trying to push his way out. Viren chuckled, finding the melodramatic gestures amusing. In other circumstances, they would have been a valiant effort in a game of charades in which the clue had been *terrified*.

"I always seem to capture the same expression," Viren said to himself. "Defiance, giving way to absolute fear."

He slipped the coin into his cloak and ascended the dungeon stairs.

CHAPTER 31
REALLY BAD NEWS

Up high in the tree, Ezran stroked the dimly glowing egg. Rayla walked over to him, her injured arm dangling by her side.

"It seems to be hanging in there," she said, pointing to the egg. "Barely."

"I'm really sorry I messed up the plan," Ezran said with a sigh. He rubbed his cheek against the egg's shell.

"Eh, you should cut yourself a break. Everybody messes up sometimes," Rayla said. She sat down next to Ezran and looked out into the forest. "Or in my case . . . all the times."

"What are you talking about?" Ezran asked. Rayla was always so surefooted and brave. He suspected she was trying to make him feel better.

"Trust me, if the plan hadn't gotten messed up when Bait flashed, I'm sure it would have flopped when it was my turn," Rayla said.

"Are you kidding?" Ezran couldn't believe what he was hearing. He turned to look Rayla directly in the eyes. "From what I can tell, you're awesome at everything."

"Well, I am pretty awesome at everything," Rayla said. Her eyes twinkled, but then her shoulders slumped. "Right up until the moment when it really matters." She hung her head. "And that's when I just . . . 'poof,' screw things up."

"Why does that happen to you?" Ezran asked.

"I don't know. I hesitate, think too much, get confused about the right thing to do. And the next thing I know, I've failed." She rolled onto her back and looked up at the stars. Ezran copied her position, so the two of them were lying head to head.

"Let me tell you a story," Rayla said. "The morning I came to your castle, my team was discovered by a human guard. It was my job to chase the guard down and stop him. But when I caught him, he looked up at me and he was so afraid. And then I just let him go. I don't know why."

"It's obvious, Rayla," Ezran said. "You felt for him. That doesn't sound like a failure to me."

"But he was a human, my enemy," Rayla said.

"Sure," Ezran said. "But he never did anything wrong to you. And when you saw he was scared, you knew he was a person. Just like you."

Rayla sighed. Ezran was too kind-hearted. He would never

understand her weakness, but she tried to explain. "It shouldn't have mattered that he was a person. I had a job to do. When I allowed that guard to escape, I endangered my whole team, people who trusted me. Then I failed at my mission. Do you realize, I'm an assassin who's never killed anyone?" she asked.

"Uh, I think that's a good thing," Ezran replied. "And by the way, thank you for failing at your mission. I like being alive."

Rayla smiled a little. "I'm glad you're alive, Ezran. Knowing you is definitely worth losing a hand." She dangled her purple hand out in front of her face.

Ezran paused, contemplating her words, then spoke up. "That's the weirdest, nicest thing anyone has ever said to me."

"Well, who knows, maybe this is my unlucky hand, so when it falls off my luck will change," Rayla said. It was an awfully dark attempt at being lighthearted.

"That's a horrible joke," Ezran said.

"Funny though?" Rayla wanted to make sure.

"Funny and horrible," Ezran conceded.

While Ezran and Rayla joked about losing limbs, Callum leaned over the edge of the cliff trying to see through the mist. As far as he could tell, the leech was circling them every minute or so, biding its time.

"I can't believe you're a mage," Ellis suddenly said. "I've never met a mage before. You're not at all what I expected."

"What were you expecting?" Callum asked, turning toward

her. Being called a mage momentarily diverted him from bigger concerns.

"Oh, you know. Taller, long robes, lots of wrinkles. Super smart," Ellis said.

Callum laughed.

"And, maybe carrying a weird amulet or something?" she added.

"Well, I am in the market for a weird amulet, if you know anybody," Callum said.

Ellis giggled. "And you're so confident."

"It's funny to hear someone say that," Callum said. He moved away from his lookout. "I don't think of myself as confident."

"Really? You should be," Ellis said. She spread her arms wide and looked up at the sky. "You have all that incredible power."

Callum paused. It didn't feel right to let Ellis believe he was so powerful. "The truth is, it's not me," he said. He pulled the primal stone out of his rucksack. "It's this. All the magic, all the power, all the confidence—it's just because of this amazing thing: a primal stone." The blue orb glinted in the moonlight, the storm inside swirling and flashing with electricity.

Ellis shook her head. "That primal stone needs you to do all that amazing stuff," she said. "Without you, it's just a neat glowy ball."

"I guess so," Callum said. "But without this, I'm nothing." He passed the stone from one hand to the other. "I'm just a guy who can draw and make wry comments from time to time. And they're not even that wry."

"I'm not convinced," Ellis said. "I have a feeling you'd be pretty amazing even without your magic ball."

Callum blushed. "Well, you seem pretty great too."

Ava barked.

"And Ava's also great," Callum said. "Is it okay if I pet her—"

Ava answered by jumping on top of Callum and lapping his face. Callum laughed.

"Hey, guys!" Rayla called out from her treetop. "I think that thing might be gone."

Sure enough, the coast looked clear, so Callum, Ellis, and Ava climbed down to meet Rayla and Ezran (and Bait) at the base of the tree.

"Haven't seen it or heard it in a while—seems like it moved on," Rayla said.

"See ya, sucker," Ezran called out. "Get it, because it's a giant leech?"

"So . . . more of a description than an insult?" Callum asked.

"Little of both," Ezran said.

Callum nodded, impressed.

"Guys, it's probably gone but let's not taunt it, okay?" Rayla said. "There's a little thing called irony, where just as you say one thing you're really sure about, that's when the opposite happens."

"Nah," Callum said. "Maybe that's how things work in stories, but in the real world—"

An earth-shattering screech interrupted Callum. The group turned around to find that the colossal leech had returned and was, once again, towering over them.

The monster reared up and prepared to strike. It lunged at the group, smashing its head into the ground and just missing everyone. Then it chased after the nearest prey, Ellis riding on Ava's back.

Ava circled around trees, evading the slithering beast, which soon turned its attention to Rayla.

Rayla scrambled up a tree and the leech switched directions again, this time focused on Ezran.

"Hey, guys," Callum called out. "The plan! The plan! We can do this." It wasn't every day Callum got a second chance at defeating the same monster, and he was not about to waste the opportunity. He pointed to Ezran, like a conductor launching a symphony, and yelled, "Ez and Bait, you're up."

Ezran hoisted Bait into the air and everyone closed their eyes. "Flash!" Callum yelled.

The blinding light stunned the leech, which stopped its attack momentarily. Then Callum pointed at Ava and called out, "Woof!"

Ava and Ellis leaped into action, riding around in circles with Ava barking madly. The leech twirled like a monstrous dancer. Here and there Ava would take a nip at the blinded leech, which became increasingly disoriented.

"Perfect," Callum said. "It's my turn for Zap." Holding the primal stone in one hand, Callum traced the lightning rune in the air and an electric charge started to build. "Here goes nothing," he said to himself, trying the powerful spell for the first time since learning the Draconic trigger word. Callum directed his hand at the leech.

"Fulminis!"

It worked. Lightning crackled out of Callum's hand, shocking the leech and sending it reeling backward. Callum's eyes widened and he gawked at his own hand.

"Yeah! Get zapped," he shouted at the leech, jumping up and down. "Get zapped by The Zapper! The most zappy and zappifying Zap Hand!" He admired his fingers again. "Wow! I can't believe it worked!"

"Uh, can you be astounded later?" Rayla asked. She gestured to the still-living monster.

"Right . . . ugh . . . finishing time," Callum said. "Rayla, you got this. Slash!"

Rayla leaped toward the disabled leech, approaching it with her blades poised as it thrashed on the ground.

But just as she was about to strike, the leech reared up again and Rayla stumbled, falling backward. She dropped her blades a few feet behind her.

Everyone watched petrified as the leech lunged at her.

Come on, Rayla, she thought. *Don't screw this up.* She crab-walked backward and reached for a blade while the leech prepared to lunge again.

"Rayla!" Callum cried out.

The beast dove toward her as Rayla grabbed her blade and sprang up from the ground.

Slash!

She beheaded the colossal leech. It crumpled to the ground, where it thumped and moaned a few times. Then it was still.

Rayla leaned over with her hands on her knees and tried to catch her breath. That was too close. If it had been a split second faster, she would have been toast. She wiped the sweat from her brow. *At least it's over now.*

Aaaaiiiieeeee! Aaaiiiieeeee!

A cacophony of ear-splitting squeals erupted from the direction of the leech.

"It can't still be alive," Rayla said, turning back around.

And she was right—the colossal leech was dead, but thousands of baby leeches were squirming out of its severed head, swarming the ground. In no time at all, they had slithered over Rayla's legs and were climbing up her body.

"Help! Help me!" Rayla shouted.

Callum sprang into action. With self-assured hands, he held the primal stone out and traced the wind-breath rune in the air.

"Aspiro!" he shouted. He took a deep breath, then blew all the tiny leeches off Rayla.

"Yes!" Callum said when the spell died down. "How 'bout that? I knew 'Whoosh' should have been part of the plan!"

CHAPTER 32
EZRAN'S GIFT

There it is. That's our tree," Ellis said. They had continued their climb toward the rim and the mist had lessened a bit. In the distance up ahead, a large lone tree stuck out from some craggy rocks. Moonlight lit up its lush leaves and wide trunk.

Ezran was tired—more than tired—but the sight of the tree gave him a burst of energy. Callum apparently got one too.

"We're almost there. We can do this, team!" Callum said. "We can make it to the rim. We're going to find the healer and save the egg!"

Just then, Ava whined and looked at Ezran with downcast eyes. Ezran put his hand on the wolf's soft fur and listened closely. But his heart broke when he heard what Ava had to say.

"Oh no," Ezran said.

"What is it?" Callum asked.

Ezran shook his head. "I have really bad news." He walked a few feet away from the group and then turned to face them. "Even if we make it to the rim, it doesn't matter. There is no miracle healer."

"What?" Rayla said. "What are you talking about?"

"Of course there's a healer," Callum said.

"No, there isn't." Ezran didn't know how he could say it more clearly.

"Why are you saying this?" Rayla asked.

Ezran looked at Ava, then back to the group. "If I told you, you wouldn't believe me."

Ellis and Rayla stared at Ezran with a mixture of sadness and confusion, but his brother glared at him coldly. After all this time, Callum still didn't understand.

"There is no miracle healer. I'm sorry," Ezran said again. He knelt beside the dimly flickering egg and stroked its shell. They had been so close.

"Stop being mysterious," Callum said. "If you're going to make a claim like that, you owe everyone an explanation."

Ezran paused. He was pretty sure his brother didn't actually want him to share his secret with the others, but since he'd brought it up . . .

"Okay," he said. "Ava told me—"

"Oh, here we go," Callum said, rolling his eyes.

"What, what is it?" Rayla asked.

"I can understand animals," Ezran said. He gave Callum a look.

"Well, did you consult Bait about the healer?" Callum asked. "Bait might disagree. Or maybe we can find an opinionated squirrel around here somewhere?"

"I knew you wouldn't believe me," Ezran said. His voice had an I-told-you-so tone but he didn't care. He plopped down on the ground and crossed his arms.

"Ezran, I'm listening to you," Rayla said softly. She knelt down next to him. "But it is pretty hard to believe. How is it that you understand animals?"

Ezran relaxed a little; Rayla sounded like she actually wanted to know. He turned and spoke only to her. "I've always been different," he said. "I don't really 'get' other kids, and it's . . . so hard for me to fit in."

"Eh. That's okay. Fitting in is overrated," Rayla said.

"But with animals? Somehow, I have this . . . connection," Ezran continued. "And a few years ago, I realized I could understand what they were saying."

Ellis had come down off Ava and was listening intently now too. Callum had walked a ways off and was kicking pebbles.

"Can you believe this?" he yelled.

"Why would Ezran lie?" Rayla shot back.

"Oh, I don't know. Because he's a kid? Because it's fun? Because he's afraid to go up the mountain?"

"I'm not afraid," Ezran said. And it was true. He knew Callum understood that too.

"Come on, Ez, tell the truth." Callum turned to the group. "Ezran made this same claim a few years ago and I asked him to prove it. He told me that a group of raccoons had told him about a treasure behind a secret waterfall. So, we followed their 'directions' perfectly." He looked at Ezran. "But when we got there, was there a treasure under the waterfall?"

"No," Ezran admitted.

"But did my underwear get soaked?" Callum asked.

"Yes," Ezran said.

"Case closed." Callum kicked a big rock.

"The raccoons were being mischievous," Ezran said. He'd told Callum that a million times. "I have since learned you cannot trust raccoons."

Callum threw up his hands. "This is ridiculous! See, Ez, this is why you can't make friends."

A lump formed in Ezran's throat. He had friends, and they were standing right here.

"Callum, back off," Rayla said firmly.

"Do you believe me, Rayla?" Ezran asked.

"Does it matter?" she said.

Ezran considered this. Yes, he decided. It did matter.

"I believe you, Ez," Ellis said. "But I also know the miracle healer is real. Because I have my Ava." She hugged the four-legged wolf.

Ezran turned to his brother, but Callum was already moving up the hill. "We need to get to the rim," he said without looking back. "We'll find out whether there's a healer when we get there."

CHAPTER 33
JERKFACE

Some while later, Callum turned the rune cube over and over in his hands as they walked. He felt a little bad he'd been so harsh on Ezran, but the stakes of their mission were high; they couldn't afford to make decisions based on little kid games. Ezran hadn't said a word to him since their fight.

He flipped the cube to the side with the Moon rune and just as he expected, it glowed.

"Huh. The higher we walk up this Caldera, the brighter the Moon rune glows," he said. He held up the cube so everyone could see.

"Here's a theory," Rayla said. "The higher we walk, the closer we are to the moon." She pointed at the sliver of moon above them.

"I don't know. Something seems different to me," Callum

said. The glow was more intense than when he held it up to Bait or Rayla.

oooooOOOOOOOOooooooo.

Callum jumped. "Ezran, cut that out," he snapped. "It's not funny."

"I didn't do anything," Ezran said.

Ellis and Ava stopped in their tracks. "Well, I heard something too," Ellis said. "Did anybody make a scary, haunted ghost sound?"

Rayla shook her head. "I didn't make it. But I definitely heard it. And I've decided I'm ignoring it. Everyone keep moving." She started back up the hill and the group followed.

oooooOOOOOOOOooooooo.

"I heard it again," Ezran said. "Maybe we should find out what it is."

No, we should not, Rayla thought. Was it too much to ask to just get to their destination? Her bad hand was throbbing more than ever.

"I'm going to share an old elven proverb with you," Rayla said, continuing to move up the slope. "When traveling up a mountain trying to save a dying dragon egg and you hear a spooky sound, just keep walking."

"Wow, that's a really specific proverb," Callum said.

Despite herself, Rayla grinned.

"What if someone needs help?" Ezran asked.

"Ez, you have a good heart," Rayla said. "It's super annoying."

But then Ezran batted his lashes and gave Rayla a wide-eyed, innocent stare.

Uggggggh. The human pipsqueak was probably right.

"Fine, but we shouldn't all go up there. I'll check it out. The rest of you stay here and keep the egg safe."

She unfurled one blade with her good hand and headed off in the direction of the moaning.

Rayla wove her way through the trees, her blade poised and her ears perked. The closer she got to the sound, the stranger the forest became. The rocks and trees around her were shrouded in sticky, weblike strings. Soon, she had to cut through the thickening web with her blade. She slashed the white mess, her good arm getting more tired with each swing.

She cut through a particularly thick mass of web and then suddenly, the moaning was louder than ever.

oooooOOOOOOOOooooooooo.

Rayla shivered at what she saw. There was a human-sized figure wrapped in webbing from head to toe, suspended in a giant net of sticky strings.

Rayla's heart was in her throat, but her fear gave way to compassion. Whatever was making that sound desperately needed their help. She approached the massive cocoon.

"Turrrrrn baaack," the unfortunate creature called out.

Startled but undeterred, Rayla stepped closer. "What did you just say?"

"Before it gets you tooooo," the voice moaned.

Rayla's heart skipped a beat, but she was not about to leave someone suffering in this state. "I'm not leaving you," she said. "Don't worry. Just hang on, I'm going to help."

Very carefully, Rayla placed her blade against the sac and cut a small slit in the webbing. She was careful that her blades would only penetrate deep enough to cut through the webs without harming whoever was inside.

But to her utter shock, the entire sac collapsed into a pile of dust. Rayla gasped. Whatever had been inside was so fragile, the moment it was exposed to air it perished. She turned and ran in the direction she had come.

As she sprinted back toward the group, she tried to shake the image of the disintegrating creature from her mind, but it played out over and over again. The voice was gone, but whoever it had belonged to, Rayla was sure she had killed it.

Get yourself together, Rayla, she thought, slowing to a jog. At least nothing had attacked her. But what would she tell the group?

By the time she joined the others, Rayla had made a decision.

"So, what was the sound?" Ezran asked.

"It was too late to help it," Rayla said. "We should get moving."

Ellis, Ava, and Ezran started up the mountain ahead of Rayla, but Callum lingered.

"Are you okay?" he asked Rayla.

The image of the sac flashed in her mind again, and for some reason, she found she wanted to share what she had seen with Callum, even if she didn't tell anyone else. "It was horrible, Callum," she said. "It was barely alive. Crumbled to dust right in front of me. Whatever it was . . . it was the prey. It's the predator we need to watch out for."

Callum nodded—that did seem to be a pattern up here. He

felt a sense of dread in his stomach, but he was glad Rayla had told him the truth.

Meanwhile, Ezran had become distracted by a rustling noise. There was the shadow of something in the trees he couldn't quite make out.

He strained his eyes to see in the darkness, gazing up into the branches. Slowly, the shadow came into focus.

"Arrrrggg!" Ezran screamed. There was a huge glowing face in the trees. It was fierce and skeletal and seemed to drip with slime.

"Ez! What's wrong?!" Callum yelled, running over to him.

But by the time he reached Ezran, the face had disappeared.

"I . . . I saw something," Ezran stammered. "But it's gone now."

Ellis nodded; she'd been in Ezran's shoes before. "Something's watching us," she said. "If you guys want to turn back, we can try to find another way to the tree."

"There's no turning back," Callum said. "The egg doesn't have much time. We press on, no matter what."

And so they pressed on. Soon, the forest became dense with the white webs Rayla had encountered earlier. Rayla sliced a path through the stickiness but it had become harder and harder to see, and the muscles in her good arm were beginning to shake.

When they ran up against a solid wall of webs, Rayla stopped.

"Can't you cut through it?" Callum asked.

"Probably better if we can go around it," she said, wary of laying waste to some monster's home.

But the web stretched far in both directions. Ava ran up and down its length, sniffing at its base.

"I don't know if there is an 'around,'" Callum concluded after a moment. "We just need to punch through."

"All right," Rayla said, seeing they had no other choice. "Let's find out what made this." She swiped through the thicket and the group entered a webbed area where everything was sticky.

"Be careful. Do not touch those webs," Rayla ordered.

"Ugh, they're everywhere . . . It's too dark," Ezran said.

CLICK.

"Everyone stop moving," Rayla said. The group froze.

But the forest was silent.

Rayla motioned for them to begin walking again.

CLICK. CLICK. CLICK. The sound came from behind them.

The hairs on the back of Callum's neck stood up. He slowly turned around.

A giant spider, easily as big as the colossal leech, stared down at them with penetrating red eyes. Its legs were as wide as tree trunks and covered in purple fur. Its abdomen was covered in a bright green pattern—the "face" Ezran had seen before.

AAAAAIIIEEEEEEEEEE! the spider shrieked.

Don't scream, don't scream, don't scream, Callum told himself. They'd defeated the leech; they would defeat this monster too. He quickly pulled out the primal stone and drew the lightning spell rune in the air. "We can do this," he said. "Fulminis!"

A lightning bolt crackled to life in his hand and he released the energy toward the monster.

But the instant the lightning touched it, the spider disappeared into thin air.

"Ah! Did I get it?" Callum asked, though he was pretty sure he hadn't. "Where'd it go? Is it in my hair?!" A shiver coursed through his body.

"Really?" Rayla asked. "It's a two-ton magical spider; you'd know if it was in your hair."

"Shh . . . we need to listen," Ellis whispered.

Callum brushed off his head one last time then began looking around every which way. He couldn't see anything, but he heard . . . scurrying? It was hard to tell. *What would a two-ton magical spider sound like if it scurried?* he wondered.

AAAAIIIIIEEEEEEEEE!

The tremendous spider suddenly dropped down from above. Callum and the others took off running and found shelter behind a hedge. The spider loomed ahead, directly in their path to the tree.

"How are we going to get past that thing?" Callum asked.

"Even if we manage to get past it, one misstep and we're caught in those crazy webs," Rayla said. "And trust me, you don't want to know what happens if you get caught in a web."

"There has to be a way. We have to get through," Callum said.

"Wait a second," Ezran said. "Something's not right."

Callum glared at his brother. There was a ginormous spider in their way. *Many* things about this situation weren't right.

But a smile slowly spread across Ezran's face. "Something's

not right in a very good way," he said. "It's going to be okay, guys. We can just walk right past it." Ezran stepped out from the hiding spot, holding Bait in his arms.

"What are you talking about?" Callum said.

Ezran stood up taller. "That monster's not real, I'm sure of it."

"That doesn't make any sense," Rayla said.

"Exactly. All those crazy chitters and screams—they don't make any sense! That's not how spiders talk."

Callum sighed. "Ezran, you've lost your mind."

"I'm going out there to prove it," Ezran said, and made a move toward the spider.

Callum grabbed his arm. "Don't."

But Ezran pulled out of Callum's grasp and ran toward the spider.

"Ezran, no!" Callum cried. He stared in horror as Ezran marched straight up to the monster and waved his arms at it. The giant spider lunged but stopped before reaching Ezran. Then it opened its grotesque, slimy maw and let out the most bloodcurdling scream Callum had ever heard. He raced toward Ezran.

Ezran looked the spider right in the face and unleashed his own most terrible roar just as Callum came up next to him. The spider didn't react.

"It's fun! Try screaming at him," Ezran said, giggling.

Callum wasn't so sure about screaming, but he held his hand out toward the spider. It roared but didn't move any closer.

"See, it won't do anything," Ezran said.

"You're right," Callum admitted. He turned to the others. "Ez is right!"

"Let's see if we can get it to turn around and show us the creepy glow face," Ezran said.

While Ezran tickled one of the spider's legs, Callum hung his head. If Ezran was right about the spider, that meant Callum was wrong about Ezran. He tapped his little brother on the shoulder. "Ez, I owe you an apology."

"Well, at least one," Ezran said.

"I'm sorry I didn't believe you," Callum said. "I promise I won't ever doubt you again."

"If you really mean it—"

"I do," Callum said, looking his brother in the eye.

"Then you have to do the thing," Ezran said.

Callum's eyes went wide. "Here? Now?" It was one thing for him to do the thing at home . . . but in front of their new friends? In front of Rayla?

Ezran nodded and Callum couldn't help himself; he smiled. The dance was actually pretty fun. Callum took a deep breath then began to dance.

He kicked his knees up in the air and crossed his arms out in front of him. He made funny faces too, which had been his idea back when Ezran and he made the deal about this silly dance being used to resolve their deepest conflicts. The faces really took things to another level.

The giant spider resumed screaming and Ezran laughed.

"It's Callum's Famous Jerkface Dance!" he called to the others. Callum hammed it up even more.

Rayla, Ellis, and Ava came out of hiding and took in both the spider and Callum's moves.

"I'm not sure which is more terrifying," Rayla said. "But if the spider is fake, then what is it? And what's it doing here?"

Ezran cheered. "I think the spider wants more dancing—knees higher! Knees higher!"

Callum danced until his stomach hurt from laughing.

With lighter hearts and high hopes, the group left the fake spider behind. They arrived at the base of the hollow tree a few minutes later. The trunk was as large as a small cottage and rose what had to be at least one hundred feet into the night sky.

"This is it!" Ellis said. "We were hiding in that tree when the miracle healer found us. It was the only shelter I could find from all the snow and monsters. Remember this place, girl?" Ava licked Ellis's face. "This way, guys." Ellis led the group into the hollow of the tree through a small triangular space, like the opening to a tent. Inside the hollow was a cavelike expanse covered in moss and fungi.

"So, now what?" Callum asked, pacing around the perimeter. "Do we just call for her? Miracle Healer! Hello. We're here." He started waving his hands in the air.

"I don't know. I just showed up, and then she showed up," Ellis said.

"Yeah, I don't see why that shouldn't work," Callum said.

But as soon as Callum had closed his mouth, a soft glow began to light the hollow.

Rayla turned toward the light, which was coming from just outside the tree. "Actually, I think it *is* working," she said. She pointed to the moon as the gang piled out of the tree hollow.

A figure seemed to emerge as if from the moon, getting larger as it approached the tree. Rayla could make out wings so broad they appeared as wide as the moon itself.

She shielded her eyes as the animal got closer, and it glided to a stop near the tree.

"It's a moon phoenix," Rayla said. She hadn't seen one since she was a small child. "It's so beautiful."

"I thought the moon phoenix was just a myth," Callum said.

"Not the first time you've been wrong today, buddy," Rayla replied.

Fair enough, Callum thought. He took in the bird's dazzling plumage. Streaks of blue and purple highlighted its thick dark feathers, which appeared iridescent and magical in the moonlight. He resisted the urge to pull out his sketchbook and begin drawing the luminous creature right then and there.

Callum watched as the phoenix knelt and a passenger dismounted. The woman sprang lightly from the bird's back. She wore a long blue cloak covered with crystals. Her snow-white hair was wound up in a knot on top of her head, and two braided plaits hung in front of her ears. Her very presence seemed to calm Callum's racing heart.

But Rayla's reaction was not calming.

"Ez was right," Rayla suddenly burst out. "That's no miracle healer. She's a fake."

"What? How do you know?" Callum asked. He'd never met a healer before, but this woman seemed gentle, like he imagined a healer would.

"She's a Moon mage, an illusionist," Rayla explained. "She can't heal anything."

CHAPTER 34
WONDERSTORM

I t's true," the Moon mage said. She placed her hand on her chest. "I am no healer. I am Lujanne, Guardian of the Moon Nexus."

Oohh, Callum thought. Then he realized he had no idea what a Moon Nexus was.

"I'm such an idiot!" Rayla said. "I should have figured it out. None of those monsters were real; they were all illusions."

"Yes," Lujanne said. "They were just to scare you. That's how I protect the Nexus."

"But...I don't understand," Ellis said. "If you're not a real healer, how did you save Ava's leg?" She placed her gloved hand on Ava's fourth leg.

Callum had been wondering the same thing. Sort of. Honestly, it was a lot to follow.

Lujanne smiled. She walked over to Ava and caressed the wolf's head. "I remember you and that little cub, both so frightened and sad," she said to Ellis. "I saw she had lost her leg. And I understood that humans would have trouble accepting her. But I knew her spirit was strong, and that was all that really mattered. To help you, I created an illusion: a leg that others would see, even though it wasn't real. I enchanted the Moonstone collar to hold the spell."

Lujanne knelt beside Ava, who was panting happily. She carefully removed the Moonstone collar. Within a few seconds, the spell cast by the collar faded and Ava's fourth leg disappeared in a twinkling yellow light. There she stood, on her three strong legs. The wolf continued to pant happily.

"She never needed that fourth leg to be happy. Everyone else did," Lujanne said.

Callum smiled. Even though Lujanne couldn't heal Ava's leg, she had helped in the way she could, and it had made all the difference to Ellis and Ava these last few years.

"But the help we need is real," Ezran suddenly said. "An illusion won't help us." He walked over to Lujanne and set down his backpack. Slowly, he lifted the flap of the bag and revealed the dragon egg. It flickered weakly.

Rayla stepped forward. "It's the egg of the Dragon Prince. It was stolen, but we saved it." She winced, realizing that even with all their efforts the egg might die after all. "I mean, we were trying to save it and return it to its mother. But there was a terrible accident—"

Lujanne interrupted Rayla with a wave of her hand. She touched the egg's shell lightly and then sighed. "Its life is fading quickly. The only chance of saving it now would be to hatch it." She frowned. "But that won't be possible. Sky dragons can only be born in the eye of a storm." She gestured around them. "The weather is clear for miles."

Rayla gazed up at the sky, her heart growing heavier by the second. There wasn't a single cloud; the moon and stars shone brightly.

"No, that can't be," Ezran said. "There has to be a way to save it."

"I'm sorry," Lujanne said.

Rayla and the others watched, crestfallen, as the dimly glowing egg finally went dark, the last of their hope fading with its light and life.

Rayla suddenly felt like she was suffocating. "I dropped the egg through the ice—this is all my fault," she said, wiping tears from her eyes.

"No, this is not your fault," Callum said. He couldn't let Rayla carry that burden alone. "I should have trusted you. Things only went wrong because we kept fighting."

"I let you both down," Rayla said. Tears continued to pour from her violet eyes. "I let the world down."

"You tried, Rayla," Ezran said, wrapping his arms around her. He was crying too. "You're so good and brave."

Callum took a deep breath, a lump rising in his throat. They had come all this way for nothing. The egg would die. The elves and humans would continue their war. There would never be peace.

A wave of grief washed over him. The feeling was familiar from the days following his mother's death, and with the thought of Queen Sarai, Callum's sadness grew; she would have been so proud if Callum and Ezran had made things right. But there was nothing Callum could do for the egg now, just as there had been nothing he could do for his mother back then. *Maybe if I were a powerful mage*, he thought, *or knew more spells to do with the primal stone—*

"Wait a minute," he said. *Sky dragons can only be born in the eye of a storm.*

A sense of certainty unlike any Callum had ever felt welled up inside him. "I know what I have to do," he announced.

He pulled the primal stone from his bag and lifted it high in the air, clouds swirling and lightning crackling within. A day ago—an hour ago, even—this orb had seemed all important to him.

But none of that mattered now.

In one swift motion, Callum smashed the stone on the ground. The orb shattered, releasing the storm it had long contained. Wind surged upward with torrential force. Blue lightning zoomed into the sky and gray storm clouds rose into the night air.

Down on the ground, the wind whirled around faster and

faster, strong as a hurricane. Everyone crouched down and gripped rocks and tree roots to resist being blown off the caldera.

But the only thing protecting the dragon egg was Ezran's backpack. A strong gust blew the precious egg from the ground, sending it somersaulting toward the edge of the cliff.

"Nooo!!" Ezran cried, reaching out his arm toward the egg.

Rayla knew this was her time to act. The egg had nearly died once because of her; she wouldn't let it happen again. She pushed herself forward, straining against the violent winds. She battled through the storm in the direction of the egg, her head down.

She was only feet away when a gust pushed the egg to the very edge of the cliff. She dove and grabbed it with her injured arm, then clutched it against her chest.

But as Rayla tried to return to safer ground, the winds picked up, hurling branches and rocks directly at her and the egg. She ducked and stayed low, covering the egg as well as she could to protect it, but the debris crashed into her arms and legs, loosening her grip on the ground. The force of the storm was punishing; she'd have to do more to stay on the mountain.

She grabbed her blade with her good hand and spiked it into the ground like a stake. The powerful winds lifted her whole body aloft, the blade the only thing keeping her from blowing away.

"Hold on, Rayla," Callum called out.

Rayla gritted her teeth as she strained against the wind.

The pain in her injured arm was worse than she had ever felt in her life, but she was determined that no force in this world would remove the egg from her protection. She closed her eyes and found the quiet place in her mind like Runaan had taught her.

Finally, finally, Rayla felt a break in the wind. She glanced above her—the eye of the storm had started to open.

A few moments later, the winds died down to create a calm space within the storm. Rayla's body came back to the ground, and Callum, Ezran, and the others were able to stand and move around, the spiraling walls of the storm rising all around them.

Above them, cracks of lightning sparked in the clouds, occasionally crossing through the eye of the storm. It wasn't long before stray lightning found contact with the egg, which was still in Rayla's arms. She saw the electricity linger within the egg, and then something began to change.

Ezran watched Rayla set the egg down carefully as it began to glow again. It grew brighter and brighter, attracting more and more lightning bolts. At first the lightning was white, like Ezran had seen many times in his life, but as the storm interacted with the egg, forks of gold and pink and teal began to appear. The egg slowly rose off the ground.

And then, to Ezran's amazement, the entire storm came alive in a spectacular rainbow of colors. He stared in awe at the wonder in the clouds, hope growing in his chest, then turned his attention back to the egg.

Crack. The sound was barely audible above the roar of the storm. A crack appeared on the egg, then another, then many more. Ezran's heart beat faster.

The cracks widened, sending beams of light streaming out into the sky. Ezran felt like he himself might burst.

Then all at once, the storm went still. The light from the egg faded, and it came to rest on the ground.

One second passed, then two. Ezran hardly dared breathe. Five seconds, six. The egg remained still. Ten seconds, twelve. When Ezran could stand it no longer, he scooped up Bait and tiptoed to the egg, afraid of what he might see—or not see.

Pop. A piece of the egg fell away. Ezran broke into a huge grin and leaned in.

A tiny blue creature strained to push its head out into the world. It yawned the cutest yawn Ezran had ever seen and broke free of the shell. Its eyes were still sealed shut and it took a few clumsy steps with its oversized paws.

"Come on, Bait, help him! His eyes are stuck," Ezran said. He nudged Bait toward the baby dragon.

Bait looked back at Ezran, utterly mortified. He had never liked baby creatures, and Ezran knew it.

"You need to lick his eyes open," Ezran insisted.

Bait begrudgingly licked the baby dragon's eyes, and in a few seconds, they started to unseal and open up.

The dragon leaped at Bait, licking him like a happy puppy, then made an affectionate sound that Ezran was pretty sure meant "Mama?" in baby Draconic.

Then the dragon hopped over to Ezran, making little dragon squeals. Ezran scooped him up and put his ear to its mouth, hardly believing he was about to communicate with a dragon.

"You know your own name!" he said a moment later. "It's Azymondias? We'll call you 'Zym.'" He turned the dragon to face Rayla, who looked relieved but was nursing her injured hand. Zym stared at her with curiosity.

"That's Rayla," Ezran said to Zym. "You almost blew off this mountain, but Rayla saved you." Hearing Ezran's words, Rayla began to weep with joy and relief.

The baby dragon bounded over to Rayla and nuzzled her injured arm. He seemed sad to see her constricted hand.

"Aw, it's okay little one," Rayla said. She scratched Zym underneath his chin. "The important thing is you—one miracle is enough for me today."

But Zym took hold of her binding between his small, nubby teeth. He tugged at it a few times, then bit down hard and pulled with all his strength. The binding snapped and the baby dragon tumbled backward.

Where magic swords, elven blades, and the sun's undying heat had been useless, the blunt teeth of this newborn dragon severed Rayla's binding.

Rayla massaged her hand, hardly believing it when life returned to her fingers. Zym pressed his cheek against hers as she wiped tears from her eyes.

CHAPTER 35
HOPE AND DANGER

Claudia and Soren ditched their horses when they hit icy ground near the top of Mount Kalik and trekked the rest of the way to the peak on foot. Claudia took a moment to survey the amazing vista, then began setting up her tracking spell on a snow-covered boulder. She unfurled a parchment map and set the jar of faintly glimmering wisps on top of it. She placed a mortar and pestle with the elf's severed braid beside the jar.

Soren watched Claudia at work, using his arms to warm himself and stop his shivering. "Couldn't you do this someplace warmer?" he asked.

"No," Claudia said, without taking her eyes off her work. "But if you like, I can use these rare components to conjure a magical blanket for you, instead of using them to locate the lost princes. You would be insanely comfortable."

"Fine. I'll suffer," Soren said.

Claudia took a flint from her pocket and lit a spark that incinerated the braid. She began chanting and purple energy seeped out of the burning hair into her fingertips. Soon, her eyes were glowing purple as well.

Claudia wrapped her hands around the jar and chanted some more, transferring the energy from her hands to the wisps. The creatures turned purple and glowed brighter. They started buzzing rapidly within the jar, with so much growing energy and intensity it seemed the jar might explode.

With a flick of her wrist, Claudia uncorked the jar and the supercharged wisps streaked out. They arced like a purple meteor across the sky, shooting off into the distance. Meanwhile, a purple line appeared on the parchment, tracing a path from Mount Kalik . . . to the Cursed Caldera.

"There! That's where we'll find them," Claudia said.

Her eyes faded to a vacant black.

Rayla, Callum, and Ezran (and Bait), along with their new friends, Ellis and Ava, sat down in a circle and watched Zym learn to walk and play. The newborn bounded around, testing out his brand-new legs, tripping over his own wings, and sniffing the cool mountain air.

As Zym played, an unusual purple light rose in the sky and shone down on the caldera.

"Look. What is it?" Ezran asked, pointing to the purple arc.

When the meteor reached a zenith above them, it burst like a firework, and thousands of tiny lights dispersed in every direction. The group danced around in the purple glow, laughing and giggling.

One of the unusual lights landed on Rayla's hand and she smiled. It was unlike any creature she'd ever seen. "They're gentle—they even tickle a little," she said. She blew the delicate creature off her hand, and Zym batted at it in the air.

Another one landed on Bait's nose and he crossed his eyes in a grumpy stare. Then he flicked his tongue out and swallowed the creature ... only to burp it back up a moment later. Everyone laughed.

Lujanne observed the merriment but didn't join in. She looked back at where the meteor had originated and furrowed her brow. The birth of the Dragon Prince had been a great miracle, but danger and darkness would soon come.

about the authors

Aaron Ehasz grew up in Baltimore, Maryland. He studied philosophy in college with the obvious goal of one day making cartoons and video games. Aaron was the head writer of the beloved series *Avatar: The Last Airbender* and is co-creator of *The Dragon Prince.*

Melanie McGanney Ehasz grew up in New York City, surrounded by books and tall buildings, and has a master's degree in English literature.

Aaron and Melanie live with three children and two fur children in Santa Monica, California, where they are surrounded by books and palm trees.